GENESIS

GENESIS

Bernard Beckett

MARINER BOOKS
HOUGHTON MIFFLIN HARCOURT
BOSTON ■ NEW YORK

First Mariner Books edition 2010

Copyright © 2006 by Bernard Beckett

First published by Longacre Press, NZ, 2006

Subsequently published by the Text Publishing Co., Australia

First published in Great Britain in 2009 by Quercus

For information about permission to reproduce
selections from this book, write to Permissions,
Houghton Mifflin Harcourt Publishing Company,
215 Park Avenue South, New York, New York 10003.

www.hmhbooks.com

Library of Congress Cataloging-in-Publication Data
Beckett, Bernard, date
Genesis / Bernard Beckett.
p.   cm.
"First published by Longacre Press, NZ, 2006"—T.p. verso.
ISBN 978-0-547-22549-4
I. Title.
PR9639.4.B434G46 2009
823'.92 — dc22   2008037387

ISBN 978-0-547-33592-6 (pbk.)

Book design by Melissa Lotfy
Text is set in Adobe Arno Pro.

Printed in the United States of America

DOC 10 9 8 7 6 5 4 3 2 1

This book is printed on 100 percent postconsumer-waste recycled stock.

Is the soul more than the hum of its parts?

—DOUGLAS HOFSTADTER, *The Mind's I*

FIRST HOUR

Anax moved down the long corridor. The only sound was the gentle hiss of the air filter overhead. The lights were down low, as demanded by the new regulations. She remembered brighter days, but never spoke of them. It was one of the Great Mistakes, thinking of brightness as a quality of the past.

Anax reached the end of the corridor and turned left. She checked the time. They would be watching her approach, or so it was rumored. The door slid open, quiet and smooth, like everything in The Academy zone.

"Anaximander?"

Anax nodded.

The panel was made up of three Examiners, just as the regulations had promised. It was a great relief. Details of the examination were kept secret, and among the candidates rumors swirled. "Imagination is the bastard child of time and ignorance," her tutor Pericles liked to say, always adding "not that I have anything against bastards."

Anax loved her tutor. She would not let him down. The door closed behind her.

The Examiners sat behind a high desk, the top a dark slab of polished timber.

"Make yourself comfortable." The Examiner in the middle spoke. He was the largest of the three, as tall and broad as any Anax had ever seen. By comparison the other two looked old and weak, but she felt their eyes upon her, keen and sharp. Today she would assume nothing. The space before them was clear. Anax knew the interview was being recorded.

EXAMINER: Four hours have been allotted for your examination. You may seek clarification, should you have trouble understanding any of our questions, but the need to do this will be taken into consideration when the final judgment is made. Do you understand this?

ANAXIMANDER: Yes.

EXAMINER: Is there anything you would like to ask, before we begin?

ANAXIMANDER: I would like to ask you what the answers are.

EXAMINER: I'm sorry. I don't quite understand . . .

ANAXIMANDER: I was joking.

EXAMINER: Oh. I see.

A bad idea. Not so much as a flicker of acknowledgment from any of them. Anax wondered whether she should apologize, but the gap closed quickly over.

EXAMINER: Anaximander, your time begins now. Four hours on your chosen subject. The life and times of Adam Forde, 2058–2077. Adam Forde was born seven years into the age of

Plato's Republic. Can you please explain to us the political circumstances that led to The Republic's formation?

Was this a trick? Anax's topic clearly stated her area of expertise covered the years of Adam's life only. The proposal had been accepted by the committee without amendment. She knew a little of the political background of course, everybody did, but it was not her area of expertise. All she could offer was a classroom recitation, familiar to every student. This was no way to start. Should she challenge it? Were they expecting her to challenge it? She looked to their faces for clues, but they sat impassive as stone, offering her nothing.

EXAMINER: Anaximander, did you understand the question?
ANAXIMANDER: Of course I did. I'm sorry. I'm just . . . it doesn't matter . . .

Anax tried to clear her mind of worries. Four hours. Plenty of time to show how much she knew.

ANAXIMANDER: The story begins at the end of the third decade of the new millennium. As with any age, there was no shortage of doomsayers. Early attempts at genetic engineering had frightened large sectors of the community. The international economy was still oil based, and the growing consensus was that a catastrophic shortage loomed.

What was then known as the Middle East remained a politically troubled region, and the United States — I will use the designations of the time for consistency — was seen by many to have embroiled itself in a war it could not win, with a culture it did not understand. While it promoted its interests

5

as those of democracy, the definition was narrow and idio-syncratic, and made for a poor export.

Fundamentalism was on the rise on both sides of this divide, and the first clear incidents of Western Terrorism in Saudi Arabia in 2032 were seen by many as the spark for a fire that would never be doused. Europe was accused of having lost its moral compass and the independence riots of 2047 were seen as further evidence of secular decay. China's rise to international prominence, and what it called "active diplomacy," led many to fear that another global conflict was on the horizon. Economic expansion threatened the global environment. Biodiversity shrank at unprecedented rates, and the last opponents of the Accelerated Climate Change Model were converted to the cause by the dust storms of 2041. In short, the world faced many challenges, and by the end of the fifth decade of the current century, public discourse was dominated by a mood of threat and pessimism.

It is, of course, easy to be wise with the benefit of hindsight, but from our vantage point it is now clear that the only thing the population had to fear was fear itself. The true danger humanity faced during this period was the shrinking of its own spirit.

EXAMINER: Define spirit.

The Examiner's voice was carefully modulated, the sort of effect that could be achieved with the cheapest of filters. Only it wasn't technology Anax heard; it was control, pure and simple.

Every pause, every flickering of uncertainty: the Examiners observed them all. This, surely, was how they decided. Anax felt suddenly slow and unimpressive. She could still hear Pericles' last words. "They want to see how you will respond to the chal-

6

lenge. Don't hesitate. Talk your way toward understanding. Trust the words." And back then it had sounded so simple. Now her face tautened and she had to think her way to the words, searching for them in the way one searches for a friend in a crowd, panic never more than a moment away.

ANAXIMANDER: By spirit I mean to say something about the prevailing mood of the time. Human spirit is the ability to face the uncertainty of the future with curiosity and optimism. It is the belief that problems can be solved, differences resolved. It is a type of confidence. And it is fragile. It can be blackened by fear, and superstition. By the year 2050, when the conflict began, the world had fallen upon fearful, superstitious times.

EXAMINER: Tell us more about these superstitions.

ANAXIMANDER: Superstition is the need to view the world in terms of simple cause and effect. As I have already said, religious fundamentalism was on the rise, but that is not the type of superstition I'm referring to. The superstition that held sway at the time was a belief in simple causes.

Even the plainest of events is tied down by a thick tangle of permutation and possibility, but the human mind struggles with such complexity. In times of trouble, when the belief in simple gods breaks down, a cult of conspiracy arises. So it was back then. Unable to attribute misfortune to chance, unable to accept their ultimate insignificance within the greater scheme, the people looked for monsters in their midst.

The more the media peddled fear, the more the people lost the ability to believe in one another. For every new ill that befell them, the media created an explanation, and the explanation always had a face and a name. The people came to fear even their closest neighbors. At the level of the individual, the community, and the nation, people sought signs of others' ill intentions; and everywhere they looked, they found them, for this is what looking does.

This was the true challenge the people of this time faced. The challenge of trusting one another. And they fell short of this challenge. This is what I mean, when I say they faced a shrinking of the spirit.

EXAMINER: Thank you for your clarification. Now please return to your story of the times. How did The Republic come to be established?

Just as Pericles had predicted, Anax was buoyed by the sound of her own voice. This is what made her such a good candidate. Her thoughts followed her words, or so he explained it. "Everybody is different, and this is your skill." So although the story she was telling was a stale one, left too long, examined too often, Anax found herself wrapping it in new words, growing in confidence with every layer.

ANAXIMANDER: The first shot of the Last War was fired in misunderstanding. It happened on August 7, 2050. The Japanese–Chinese alliance had spent eighteen months trying to piece together a coalition to oversee the sulfur-seeding project, in the hope that the heat-trapping effects of atmospheric carbon could be countered. That the coalition was unable to advance was due largely to the distrust I have mentioned. The U.S. blocked the initiative, believing it was part of a greater plan to establish a new international order, and China in turn believed the U.S. was deliberately accelerating climate change in order to crush the Chinese economy. In the predictable way these things unfold, China set about a plan for a secret unilateral action.

The plane shot down over U.S. air space in the Pacific was engaged in the first of the seeding trials, although as we all know, the U.S. never wavered from its official line that it was a military plane engaged in hostile actions.

EXAMINER: It is better you assume we know nothing.

Anax bowed her head in apology, feeling her cheeks glow with shame. She waited for a signal to continue but none came. In any other circumstance she would have railed against their rudeness.

ANAXIMANDER: Plato's power base came from his global economic interests. He made his initial fortune in hydrogen technology, and compounded this with wise investments in the biocleansing industry. With his wealth and contacts, Plato was better placed than most to foresee the likely outcome of an escalating conflict between the superpowers. Always a prudent man, he began to move his money to a group of islands at the bottom of the world known then as Aotearoa. By the time war was declared, he and his associates were said to own seventy percent of the island economy, and were already moving it toward a state of technology-rich self-sufficiency. As the international situation worsened, Plato found it a simple matter to convince the people of his adopted homeland of the need for a more effective defense system. What is still regarded as the twenty-first century's finest engineering feat, the Great Sea Fence of The Republic, was completed by 2051, eleven months into the Last War.

By the time the first plague was released at the end of 2052, The Republic was already sealed off from the world. Plato was revered as the savior of Aotearoa, and, as the reports from the outside grew grimmer, he became known also as the savior of the human race itself. By the time the last external broadcast was picked up, in the June of 2053, it was widely believed within The Republic that theirs was the planet's last habitable homeland.

The refugees were expected, of course, and when they came they were dispatched. Approaching aircraft were shot down without any attempt at communication, and in the early days the people gathered on cliff tops to watch the spectacle of ghost ships exploding on the horizon as they drifted through the mined zone. Over time, the explosions became less frequent, and the laser guns were offered fewer airborne targets. It was then the people turned to Plato and asked him to take them forward, to better times.

EXAMINER: A fair summary, Anaximander. And this then is The Republic into which your subject of special interest, Adam Forde, was born. Before we get on to his extraordinary life, can you please tell us a little about the Republic Plato constructed?

ANAXIMANDER: Historians say that The Republic was best understood by its motto "Forward toward the past." Plato, or perhaps we should say Plato's advisers, for most now believe Helena to have been the key architect of The Republic's social order, preached a new style of conservatism. Plato told the people that the Downfall had come about because people had strayed from their natural state. They had embraced change uncritically, forgetting the most fundamental law of science, that change means decay. Plato told the people of The Republic that they could return to the glory of the great civilizations only by creating a society based upon stability and order.

Plato identified what he called the five great threats to order: Impurity of Breeding, Impurity of Thought, Indulgence of the Individual, Commerce, and The Outsider. His solutions were radical, but the people were frightened and clung to his many promises. "The state has saved you," Plato told them, "and now you must toil to save the state."

The people were divided into four distinct classes, based upon genomic readings: Laborers, Soldiers, Technicians, and Philosophers. Children were separated from their parents at birth, and details of their parentage were never divulged. At the end of their first year each child was tested, and either allocated to their class or terminated.

All children were subject to a rigorous education, both physical and intellectual. Wrestling and gymnastics were compulsory, along with mathematics and genetics. In the summer months the children went naked, as this was thought to lessen the desire for individuality.

The best athletes were able to advance from Laboring to Soldiering classes, even if their genomes did not predict it, and similarly the best thinkers were given the opportunity to rise to the Technician class, but never any further. The class of Philosophers was reserved for the anointed few.

Men and women lived separately, eating and sleeping in their working communes. Romance was allowed, and once couples had received clearance from the Department of Genetic Variation they were encouraged to marry. But even after marrying, they remained living among their own kind, and had to earn share-time allowances.

That I think is a fair summary of the major aspects of early Republican society.

Anax realized there would be no signs of approval from the panel, but nevertheless she could not help looking up at them, in the way a child in her first week of school might look at her instructor. If not for encouragement, then at least acknowledgment. But this wasn't school. This was The Academy.

EXAMINER: Who is your tutor, Anaximander?
ANAXIMANDER: Pericles. Mostly. I've had help in the school, of course, and I have done a lot of my own research, but —
EXAMINER: Pericles.

The Examiner said the name as if it had a special power over him. Anax could not tell if this was good or bad. She waited for the next question, hoping that soon they would get to the material with which she was most confident, the remarkable life and times of Adam Forde.

EXAMINER: In your own judgment, was Plato successful in achieving his aims?
ANAXIMANDER: That would depend upon what you take his aims to have been. If what he sought was his own personal power and stature, which I think is a fair estimate of his motivations, then at least for as long as he lived, he was able to exert considerable influence. If, however, you are asking whether he was successful in producing an ideal state, one in which the people and the society were best able to realize their potential, then it is harder to know. Perhaps history

would have found it easier to judge Plato if Adam Forde had never been born.

Just saying the name relaxed her. For three long years, Adam had never been far from her mind. Although he died long before she was born, Anax felt she knew him as well as she knew anyone. She had studied so many transcripts, downloaded so many traces, but more importantly, she had what Pericles called "the feel for him." If she couldn't impress the Examiners now, then she couldn't impress the Examiners. And that — well, she wouldn't think about it. She had promised Pericles she wouldn't think about it.

EXAMINER: Yes, Adam.

Anax was yet to meet anyone who could say the name without pausing at its significance. The new thinkers were revising his importance downward now. "There need be nothing special about the match that lights the fire," was their motto, "save that it is the match that lights the fire." But they too paused when they said his name.

EXAMINER: Anaximander, the first thing I need to hear is a little about Adam's background. Who were his parents, what were his early years like? Everyone knows about the night on guard duty, every young one can tell us the story word for word, but Adam's life didn't begin on that night. Tell us how, in your view, he got there.

ANAXIMANDER: Adam was born in the year 2058. He was raised in the Tana nursery for the first year. Legend has it that his mother had devised a method of marking her baby and had herself transferred to his nursery so that she could watch over him during that time, but it is almost certainly just a story. The myth of causation again. For those who wish to understand what it was that made Adam the way he was, the answer "everything, and therefore nothing" does not rest easy.

What we do know is that Adam was born into the Philosopher class. At the end of his first year, he underwent the normal physiological testing and had his genome read. His learning status was confirmed but a warning was placed on his file. At least two genetic markers flagged a possible unpredictability in his behavior. In fact, the legendary Clark memorandum suggested that termination be considered. In normal circumstances he would have been submitted to retesting in two months' time. But 2059 was the time of the second great plague scare, and when Clark died all her possessions were destroyed as a precaution, so the retesting order was never put on file. By the time the mistake was discovered, Adam had passed his first verbalization tests and termination was no longer a consideration. In the confusion surrounding Adam's file, the warning markers were overlooked, and the information was never passed on to the schooling bodies.

EXAMINER: So he entered straight into the Philosophers' stream?

ANAXIMANDER: Yes. The records tell us he was a top scholar who impressed immediately, particularly in mathematics and logic. He also excelled in wrestling and, at the age of thirteen, represented his city at the annual tournament. It was there we first note a display of the individuality that was to lead inevitably to his greatest role.

At the tournament he met a girl called Rebekah, a fellow wrestler, and he decided the two of them should be friends.

That they did not live in the same city or even on the same island did not deter him. On the last night of the tournament, Adam hid himself among Rebekah's team's luggage. He managed to travel seven hundred kilometers south of his allocated zone and, with Rebekah's help, avoid detection for three days before a cook discovered him hiding in the dry-food store of Rebekah's commune.

Adam was returned home with a black mark against him and, it might be said, the pattern had been set. He had shown himself to be combative, impulsive, unafraid of censure, and drawn toward female company. Normally such a transgression would see a child transferred automatically to the laboring classes but his teacher made a special plea on Adam's behalf, citing what she saw as his potential. As a concession he was transferred to an elite soldiering academy of the Republican Guards. And as a result of that decision, perhaps we can say history changed forever.

EXAMINER: If we were to believe in simple causes.

Again Anax was forced to blush at such a simple mistake. She had heard a rumor that no candidate was allowed more than two such errors. But then she had heard many rumors. This was no time for thinking such things. She had let herself become carried away by the story. Pericles had warned her this might happen. She resolved to temper her comments.

ANAXIMANDER: And of course we don't. Sorry.

None of the Examiners acknowledged her apology. Anax wondered what it would take to draw some sort of response from them. Were they like this in their homes?

EXAMINER: Tell us about the circumstances of Adam's arrest.

ANAXIMANDER: Adam was by this time seventeen years old. The year was 2075. He had graduated with distinction from the Soldiering academy, where his love of physical activity continued.

You have asked me to move to the arrest, so I will only note in passing that by graduation he had accumulated four black marks on his training record, and it was for this reason that his first posting was to a watchtower on the southern coastline of the northern island. By this time, there were very few confirmed sightings of ghost ships, and it was not thought that there was any real danger of attempted refugee landings.

The real excitement was to the north where there had lately been three unconfirmed sightings of a new type of airship. Sentries had reported a blimplike object hanging low above the horizon near sunset, and although The Republic's media were tightly controlled, rumors had spread quickly. As a precaution the top Soldiers were moved to the north, and laser-gun and strike-plane training intensified. Meanwhile Soldiers like Adam, fresh from school and with a compromised record, were left to man the remote watchtowers sprinkled along the southern coast.

Adam had been in his job for exactly seven months without incident. At his trial he reported being deeply bored by the experience, and it is likely this was no exaggeration.

The sentries worked in pairs and their routines were strictly prescribed and monitored. Each watchtower consisted of a small observation box perched atop a high metal frame, surrounded by electrified fencing and accessed by a single ladder.

The boxes themselves were small, with barely enough

room for the two sentries to turn about. Their job was a simple one, to monitor the long unbroken line of the Great Sea Fence, a huge metal mesh fence set fifty meters out past the low-tide mark. The fence climbed thirty meters above the ocean. It was topped with razor wire and guarded by small floating mines. Should anyone or anything be seen to be approaching the fence from the outside world, the sentries' duty was unambiguous.

If it were a vessel of significant size, which was unlikely as most of those were dealt with by the roving satellite-guided mines of the outer defenses, the sentries were to raise the alarm. Within five minutes, laser-armed helicopters would be hovering over it, and any disease it might have carried would be evaporated.

For the smaller, more common vessels — which drifted toward the fence from time to time, usually with no more than two or three emaciated souls on board — the sentries' task was more demanding. They were instructed to notify the station of the sighting, and then one of them would leave the watchtower and follow the path toward the firing post. There, a small-scale laser, armed with a random code memorized each morning by the sentry, would be used to obliterate the craft.

The second sentry would remain in the watchtower and was ordered to keep his gun trained on the back of the shooting sentry's head. The instructions were uncompromising. Should the first sentry show any sign of hesitation in carrying out his duties, he was to be shot immediately, without recourse or investigation. In sentry circles it was well known that many a dispute between sentries was ended in this manner, and only the foolish argued with their watch partner.

EXAMINER: And what was the nature of the relationship between Adam and his sentry partner?

ANAXIMANDER: All conversations between sentries were monitored and recorded, and so we have some idea of the dynamic between Adam and his watchtower partner, Joseph. I should add, here, that the sentries were compelled to undertake a variety of computer-prompted routines during their watch, in order to keep themselves alert. For instance, they might have to correct altered computer images against the scene ahead of them, or memorize and repeat elaborate computer-generated prompts and instructions. I tell you this, because with your permission I would like to reproduce a conversation between Joseph and Adam, recorded the day before the initial incident.

EXAMINER: If you think it helps answer the question.

Anax paused. Pericles had assured her it was a good idea, even though such memorizing was a simple trick and many of the examination manuals advised against wasting time on it. Were they trying to warn her off it? Best not to wonder. She would take Pericles' advice. She would do him proud.

ANAXIMANDER: This was recorded at 18.40, two hours into the eight-hour shift.

  J: You see anything?
  A: Yeah.
  J: What?
  A: [*Voice raised*] A ship, bigger than a mountain, making its way toward the fence. And now, it's raising itself up out of the water, oh my God, it can fly, we've got

ourselves a flying ship, it's got guns, they're aimed
right at our heads, oh my God, we're all gonna die!

J: Okay, just asked. You know they record these conversations, right?

A: Nobody listens to them.

J: How do you know that?

A: You think, if they'd been monitoring the crap I speak,
someone wouldn't have said something by now?

J: Hey man, you're flashing.

A: I know.

J: You have to hit yellow now, then orange.

A: Yeah, I'm waiting.

J: Now, before it gets too complicated to remember.

A: Orange then blue, then green, and now, wait for it, two
oranges. I think I can cope.

J: [*Agitated*] Press it, man.

A: You press it.

J: I'm not allowed. They're your buttons.

A: Who's going to know?

J: I will.

A: Go ahead.

J: I don't remember it!
[*A buzzing sound can be heard.*]

J: That's the ten-second warning! Adam, this isn't fair.
We both get punished. You know how it works.

A: We're not going to get punished.

J: Hit the lights.

A: Okay, okay. [*Slow, teasing*] I'm hitting the lights.
Yellow, orange, blue, green, orange, orange, green,
yellow, and was it red, was it green, did you see?

J: I'll shoot you. I will.

A: Red.

[*The buzzing stops.*]

A: See, nothing to worry about.

J: Why do you always do that?

A: I get bored. It helps me stay alert.

[*A long silence. Tapping at keyboards can be heard.*]

J: You think there's anything out there anymore?

A: How long you been doing this?

J: Five years.

A: How many you had to shoot?

J: Three or four. But they're just drifters. I meant, you know . . .

A: They say they've seen new airships lately, up north.

J: I thought that was just a story.

A: Everything's just a story.

J: When you think about it, how long's it been since the plague? The ones left have to have immunity, right? So they could be rebuilding. It makes sense.

A: Or they're just taking a long time to die.

J: The last ones I saw, they didn't seem that sick.

A: You know they record these conversations, right?

J: [*Worried*] You said they didn't listen to them.

A: Unless something happens.

J: What sort of something?

A: I could go mad and shoot you.

J: Then it makes no difference to me, them listening or not.

A: So nothing to worry about.

J: You think they're rebuilding, then?

A: You ever wonder how come the people we are sent down to shoot never shoot back? I think the war and

20

the plague wiped out a thousand years of progress.
I think the new airships they're seeing are just big
balloons. I think that's all they can do.

J: You know what I feel like right now?

A: What?

J: A Coke.

A: I'm not so mad on it.

J: How can you not be? You must have had it, at the
ceremonies. You must have tasted it.

A: It's just a drink.

J: You know, they almost lost the recipe. It was only in
the very last hour, before the links went down, that
anybody thought to get hold of it. Everybody just
assumed someone else knew.

A: You're too gullible. It's just a drink.

J: It's not just a drink . . . So what do you feel like?

A: A woman.

J: A woman?

A: Right here, right now. You could watch. How often do
you see your wife?

J: You know we're not allowed to discuss it.

A: We're not allowed to do a lot of things, Joseph. You
know what? I bet I spend more time with women than
you do, and I'm not even married.

J: That's just big talk.

A: Yeah, that's right, Joseph. Big talk.

And that's where the fragment of recovered transcript ended.

EXAMINER: And what do you think this shows us?

ANAXIMANDER: It shows us something of his character.

EXAMINER: Something admirable?

ANAXIMANDER: Something important.

EXAMINER: Why is it any more than idle chatter? Two bored men passing the time.

ANAXIMANDER: It reveals personality.

EXAMINER: Explain that.

ANAXIMANDER: Adam is the junior guard. Joseph is five years his senior and has greater experience, yet, listening to the conversation, you would assume the opposite is true. Adam, I think, assumes superiority in any situation. It is important to note this. It is part of the trouble.

EXAMINER: Tell us what happened next.

ANAXIMANDER: Next was the day of the sighting. According to records, Joseph and Adam began their shift at 15.30. The day was warm and clear. The sea was calm. Their watchtower was built above a cliff face, with views across the strait to the southern island. Their monitoring region extended along a range of ten nautical miles. On a day like this, it was possible for them to see the next watchtower to the north without the aid of a viewing device. According to the log, Joseph was on watch while Adam monitored the equipment, although it is Adam who noted the first sighting.

A: Well, here we go, a break in the weather.

J: What are you on about now?

A: Eyes right, little partner. See it?

J: See what?

A: They test your eyes before they put you on this detail?

J: My eyes are fine.

A: Must be a brain problem, then.

J: Okay, now I see it. [*Voice rising*] I see it!

A: Okay, settle.

J: Sound the alarm.

A: It's tiny.

J: I don't know.

A: Check your screen, you idiot.

J: You know I've got bullets in this, right?

A: You know threatening a fellow Soldier is treason?

J: They'd forgive me.

A: No, it's tiny. Be lucky if there were more than two or
three in there. Lucky you didn't waste those bullets
on me.

J: It's your turn. Check the roster.

A: Even better.

The two men's eyes flickered from their surveillance
screen to the scene in front of them and back again. The image solidified. It was indeed a small boat, just as the scanner
had indicated. A communication line from the southernmost
watchtower crackled through.

W: You boys getting that?

J: Sure, Ruth, she's all ours.

W: Go get 'em.

A: It's just the one.

J: Be careful of that. There might be others hiding.

A: When have you ever heard of any of them hiding?

J: It could happen. That's what I'm saying. You all
loaded? Away you go then. I got your back.

A: Wait a sec.

J: You have to go.

23

A: I just want to see what I'm dealing with.

J: I'll let you know if I see anything surprising.

A: Just a second.

Adam stayed staring at the screen. It was against regulations. The assigned shooter had to leave the watchtower before the victim had been identified. By the time the Soldier saw what it was he was dealing with, he had to know there was a gun aimed at the back of his head. It made perfect sense. It didn't matter how good the training was, there would always be a chance the Soldier would hesitate when it came to shooting a helpless victim. And in a time of plague the state couldn't take chances.

J: [*His hand slipping to his gun*] You know what my orders are.

A: Oh my God, look, it's a girl. It's just a little girl. Where the hell has that come from?

Both of them stared at the screen. The boat was indeed tiny. It was difficult to believe it could have made the journey from the nearest land. Adam saw her eyes. That's the way he explained it to the court. Huge and frightened, staring uncomprehendingly at the great metal barrier rearing up out of the ocean. The makeshift triangular sail of her small craft was tattered and useless. The boat bobbed dangerously close to the floating explosives.

J: [*Voice shaking*] Man, please, get out of here. I don't want to have to shoot you.

A: Joseph, there's something I should have told you.

24

J: What?

A: I've never done this before.

J: But I've seen your file.

A: I got it changed.

J: How?

A: It's best you don't know that.

J: Okay, so this is your first. Don't worry. It's not too hard. It's just like training. Once you've got the target locked on, you don't even have to watch it.

A: I don't think I can.

J: I don't think you have a choice.

A: She's just a girl.

J: I will shoot you if I have to.

A: Let me watch.

J: What are you talking about?

A: You go. I'll watch. I can't explain, I just think it'll be easier that way. If I watch this one then I'll be able to do the next one. I know I will. Come on, you know it's got to be easier than shooting me.

Joseph agreed. Easier to shoot the stranger, half-dead anyway and possibly carrying the plague, than shoot his colleague in cold blood there in that little room. And that was the only option. Adam knew this. He told the court he knew this is how it would happen. Much was made, in the media, of his cold-blooded calculations.

EXAMINER: Is that what you think? Do you think it was cold blooded?

At last, a question Anaximander could answer fully. This was her area of expertise.

ANAXIMANDER: There are two ways of interpreting what happened next, although Adam himself insisted that the version he gave at the time of his arrest is all there is to know.

He sat in the watchtower, and trained his sights on the shooting site, as per the manual. He watched Joseph arrive at the laser gun and line up the small vessel. He had never seen a kill before and while a part of him wanted to look away, he could not deny the grisly fascination. He watched Joseph closely, observed the entering of the security code and the arming of the laser. And then, following procedure, Adam checked the viewing screen, to ensure the inhabitants of the craft posed no immediate danger to his colleague. And so again he looked into her eyes, and this time he couldn't look away. She was sixteen years old, only a year younger than he was, but aged by three months at sea; out of food and water, thin and close to death.

Adam zoomed in on her face. Surveillance records confirm this. He saw her expression; confused, uncomprehending, only dimly taking in the great barrier, the fatal end of her journey.

Adam said it came to him as a flash, a realization. He told the authorities that he did not make the decision to fire, but rather heard the report of his gun echo through the small room. He looked to the laser mount, and saw his colleague slumped forward, a burn hole in the back of his head.

Immediately a message from control crackled through. By this time Adam was panicking.

"Gunshot recorded. Please report. Please report."

"This is Adam. Joseph is dispatched. We have a small vessel at the fence. There's a girl on board. Joseph hesitated, Sir."

"You're sure it's a single passenger?"

"Yes, Sir."

"You need to finish this, Adam."

"I know, Sir."

"Report back when it is done. We'll send in a substitute. Congratulations, Adam. The Republic thanks you."

"Thank you, Sir."

Adam knew time was against him. They would be waiting for the laser discharge.

He raced past his fallen colleague and scrambled down the narrow track toward the ocean. He could see the small boat, adrift and in danger of bumping against a mine. Adam waved to get the girl's attention. He had no idea if she could hear him or even if they spoke the same language.

"Can you swim?" he called. "Can you swim?"

She looked at him, but said nothing. She was too distant for him to make out the expression on her face.

He called again. "You have to get out of the boat. Swim that way. Swim north!" He pointed. "I'll come and meet you, farther along. There's a place where I can get you through. A small gate. Wait at the gate. Whatever you do, don't touch the buoys. Can you understand me? I have to destroy your boat. Please, wave if you understand me."

He watched, waiting desperately for a response. Nothing. He waved again. She waved back, a small, ambiguous gesture. Hoping against hope that she had heard him, Adam clambered back to the shooting station. The laser was still armed. He pushed Joseph aside and checked the sight. He could no longer see the girl. Had she understood his instructions, or simply slumped forward in exhaustion? There was no way of telling. He fired, and watched the hiss of steam and bubbling of water as the small craft was vaporized.

Adam called the watchtower. The communication was somber; his voice was shaking. "This is Adam, watchtower 621N. Task complete. Vessel destroyed."

"Congratulations, Adam. The substitute will be there in ten minutes. Stay where you are. We will deal with the body."

"Thank you, Sir."

But Adam didn't stay where he was. All along the sea fence there were small service gates. They worked off a remote locking device and theoretically could only be opened with simultaneously entered codes: one from the service technician on the site, the other from the central control at defense headquarters.

Adam knew the system could be overridden, although at first he insisted it was simply a case of a malfunctioning gate. There has been much controversy about how he got this information, but it is worth remembering that Adam was curious and clever, and I do not find it difficult to believe that he picked up information during his training that would not come the way of a normal Soldier.

Others have noted Adam's popularity with women, and in a society where all relationships were to be conducted covertly, it is entirely possible that he came by his information in this way. Most fancifully, some historians have noted that Rebekah, his friend from wrestling, went on to become an expert in electronic security. Some have speculated that the two may have stayed in touch, although no evidence of this ever emerged.

Whatever the method, Adam was able to open the service gate. He ran along the rocky shore, and swam out to the fence. This was by no means a simple task. Even though the sea was unusually calm that day, the gates were placed on the most inaccessible stretches of the fence-line.

Adam said that at first he thought he was too late. The girl was clinging to the other side of the fence, but she had sunk into the water and her head was down. He told us about the moment she looked up, their eyes meeting through the mesh. He described dragging her through the gate and swimming her back to the shoreline. She didn't speak, but now — as a result of her not being in the boat — he knew she understood him.

He took her to a small cave in the base of a cliff, where she could be safely hidden. He gave her a ration bar from his belt and promised to return. She leaned back against the stones, and before she closed her eyes, she smiled her thanks to him. Or at least, this is how he told it.

The substitute found him in the shooting nest, soaked to the skin, slumped over his dead friend, howling. The substitute, whose name was Nathaniel, was a goodhearted man nearing the end of his service years. He assumed the young guard had broken under the strain of carrying out his orders, and agreed to keep what he had seen to himself. Adam thanked him and continued the shift.

That night he returned to the cave, this time with water, food, and blankets. Over the next day he nursed the traveler back to a state of health where she could sit up, and in faltering English, tell him the story of her past.

EXAMINER: You said before that there are two versions of this story. Tell us more about the second.

ANAXIMANDER: From the outset, investigators were suspicious of Adam's story: his thorough knowledge of the gate security and terrain below the cliff face, the plausibility of the story he presented to the substitute, the way in which he manipulated Joseph. There were those who suggested that the entire action was premeditated and that the arrival of the traveler had been planned in advance. In the shock that followed the announcement that the security perimeter had finally been breached, the most complex and paranoid theories were advanced.

EXAMINER: But you discount them?

ANAXIMANDER: I do.

EXAMINER: Why?

ANAXIMANDER: History has shown us the futility of the conspiracy theory. Complexity gives rise to error, and in error we grow our prejudice.

EXAMINER: You sound like Pericles.

ANAXIMANDER: The words may be his, but the sentiments are my own. In Adam's case, I think it is better that we believe it happened as he told it. A simple human reaction to an unfolding situation. Conspiracy theory would have us believe it could not have happened any other way. That the whole event was premeditated and controlled. But the vessel was a small and battered single mast. How did it find its way to just the right watchtower at just the right time? And how was the detailed information needed for this feat ever conveyed? No reasonable method has ever been suggested. Although the reaction of the central control to the incident was largely procedural, there was much room for variation. The availability of substitutes dictates the time taken for them to arrive. It took fifteen minutes, but it could just as easily have been two minutes, or an hour. If he'd had a chance to plan it, Adam would

30

have had food and clothing and medical supplies waiting for the arrival of the girl, but we know it was, in part, his hurried purchasing of this equipment the next day that triggered suspicions. No, I believe it happened as Adam told us. He looked into her eyes, and he felt he had to act.

EXAMINER: And did he?

ANAXIMANDER: Did he what?

EXAMINER: Did he have to act?

ANAXIMANDER: I think that's something on which every individual has to form their own opinion.

EXAMINER: A drifting stranger arrives from a land known to have been exposed to the most devastating plague in human history. There are strict instructions regarding correct procedure. And on an emotional whim, Adam chooses to kill his friend and risk the safety of his entire community. Can we clarify, please, that you believe there is more than one way of judging these actions?

Anax hesitated. She was not prepared for this line of questioning. Her specialist subject was history, not ethics. She could explain the process by which the evidence had been painstakingly put together as Adam's story, but she could not propose a method by which that story should be judged. She had her own opinions, of course. Everybody did. Who hadn't had this discussion, in their homes, their schools, their entertainment centers? But she wasn't prepared to defend them, not on the record. She wasn't qualified to defend them. Pericles had told her to answer each question as fully and truthfully as she could. He had told her they would try to unsettle her. That they would surprise her with the angles they took. She proceeded with the greatest care.

ANAXIMANDER: I think it is well known that there is a range of sympathies across the community. And I don't think this should surprise us, given the prominent place Adam holds in our history. I think it is understandable, that some would interpret his actions as heroic. I think there is an urge in us to do this.

EXAMINER: And do you have that urge?

ANAXIMANDER: I am saying we all have that urge. Your question, I think, is whether I consider it an urge to be embraced or one to be controlled. Adam felt a sense of great empathy for the helpless traveler. He had been instructed to put that empathy aside, and the reasons for that instruction were sound. While he may have believed the threat of plague had passed, it was unreasonable for him to take it upon himself to make such a decision on behalf of the nation. He was no expert in virology. Nevertheless, I believe those who feel the urge to understand Adam's heroism instinctively understand the importance of empathy. For a society to function successfully perhaps there needs to be a level of empathy that cannot be corrupted.

For the first time the change in all three Examiners was perceptible. They straightened. The leader loomed taller, their eyes burned more intensely.

EXAMINER: Are you saying a society wracked by plague is preferable to one wracked by indifference?

ANAXIMANDER: That is a good way of framing the question.

EXAMINER: And your answer?

ANAXIMANDER: I think, in the circumstances, it is impossible to justify the romanticism of Adam's actions, although, given our history, we all have cause to be thankful for them.

Silence. They wanted her to say more, but Anax knew she had dodged a bullet and stood quietly before the panel, determined not to step back into its path.

EXAMINER: An interesting answer.

ANAXIMANDER: It was an interesting question.

EXAMINER: You will have been following the time carefully, I am sure. The first hour of the examination is now complete. From time to time, we will ask you to step outside into the waiting room, so that the panel can further plan the direction of the interview.

ANAXIMANDER: And you would like me to do that now?

EXAMINER: If you don't mind.

ANAXIMANDER: And in terms of time?

EXAMINER: The clocks will be stopped.

FIRST BREAK

FIRST BREAK

Anax felt the doors slide open behind her. Another unexpected development. *One down, three to go,* she told herself. *Stay calm.* A guard stood at the waiting-room door, to make sure she made no attempt to communicate with the outside world, she assumed. He was older than her. She looked at him and smiled. He turned away.

Anax tried to use the time to her advantage. Truth was, the break had come at just the right moment. She had lied to them. She didn't know it until she was forced to say it aloud, and the feeling was so strange she doubted it had gone unnoticed. Yes, Adam's actions were romantic, irrational, unjustifiable. And yet, when forced to comment, Anax had spoken a lie.

She did not know whether she would have done the same thing had she been up in the watchtower, she just knew Adam wasn't wrong to have done it. She tried to swallow back this new and dangerous knowledge and focus on what was coming next: surely the details of Adam's arrest and subsequent trial. She reminded herself she was prepared. She reminded herself how much success meant to her, how much it would mean to see Pericles' face when she delivered the news.

"Do you know how long they're going to be?" Anax asked, after half an hour had passed with no word being sent through. The guard turned to her. From his expression, she could see he had not been expecting her to speak.

"How should I know that?" His voice was surprisingly soft and quiet. Not like a guard's at all.

"I just thought, if you did this often . . ."

"I've never been here before," he told her. "It's my first time."

"But you are watching me?"

"What?" Confusion tightened his features.

"You're a guard, right? You're here to make sure I don't try to communicate."

"How could you?" he replied. "The building is under full surveillance. All electronic traffic is tied down."

"I know. I just thought you might be an extra precaution."

The guard began to laugh.

"What?" Anax demanded. "What's so funny?"

"I thought the same thing about you," he told her.

Now she noticed the second door. "So you're . . ."

"Yeah, through there."

"How's it going?"

"I don't know. I wasn't expecting the breaks."

"No. It's unnerving, isn't it?"

"A little."

"I'm Anax, by the way."

"Pleased to meet you. Soc."

"What's your specialist topic?"

"Do you think we should be discussing this?"

38

"Would they have put us in the same room, if they didn't want us to?"

"Perhaps they're watching," Soc suggested.

Anax liked him. She was good on first impressions. His manner was gentle. He was kind, she felt sure of it. "Have your questions been difficult?" Anax asked.

"Most have been okay," he replied. "I was thrown by a question on ethics. It's not my specialty. Perhaps that's saying too much."

"I had the same thing," she told him.

This news seemed to come as some relief to him. Soc looked at Anax as if trying to read her. He leaned forward quickly and Anax, in her surprise, pulled away. He lowered his voice so that it was little more than a hum.

"Be careful," he murmured. "They know more than you think."

He pulled back and looked at her, but she did not answer. He was a stranger to her. Who did he think he was, taking a risk like that? At just that moment, as if to underline the danger, her door slid open.

SECOND HOUR

Anax walked quietly back toward the door, avoiding Soc's eyes. She looked up at the Examiners, feeling even more nervous than before. For all she could tell, they had not moved at all. She tried to imagine what it was they had been talking about.

The Head Examiner waited for her to move into place and then went straight into the next question, as if the break had happened only in her imagination.

EXAMINER: What were the circumstances that led to Adam's arrest?

ANAXIMANDER: If anything, the details of Adam's apprehension are anticlimactic. As I have already said, there was much about his behavior to suggest that his actions in saving the girl, who for obvious reasons has become known as Eve, were spontaneous rather than planned.

As is the case with any enforced execution, the records from the watchtower in the period leading up to Joseph's

43

death were examined and the switching of duties during the incident immediately raised a warning.

Experts were sent in to examine the sea fence and they noted evidence of tampering. Adam's supply procurement transactions were monitored and, although he made the effort to secure the extra food and water using a stolen registration card, he was put under full surveillance. His tracking chip was activated, and the next night when he crept out of the dormitory, a full quarantine and enforcement team followed his every movement.

EXAMINER: Does it not seem unusual to you that a person of Adam's technical proficiency should not be aware of the tracking chips?

ANAXIMANDER: There is much speculation regarding Adam's motivation at this point. Again, the problem with conspiracy theories is their assumption that people are capable of exerting sophisticated control over events. I believe that complexity emerges quickly and unexpectedly. It is better to understand the Adam of this time as a frightened man. He has done what he believes to be right, and now finds his world spinning out of control.

EXAMINER: A romantic interpretation.

ANAXIMANDER: No, a pragmatic one. Adam was stumbling. He knew there was no one he could turn to and yet, having made his choice, he was now responsible for the life of the young girl he had saved. So, thoughtlessly, he led the security forces to the cave where she was hiding, and they swooped.

EXAMINER: What happened in that cave?

ANAXIMANDER: I doubt we can ever know for sure. The security forces were under strict instructions to bring in both

44

Adam and Eve alive, such was the concern that they were playing a part in a larger plot.

The official defense report suggests that a clever ambush had been laid. I hardly need to point out though that the forces had considerable motivation to promote this interpretation. The alternative would suggest that they had not expected the cave to be branched, and simply launched their attack down the wrong tunnel.

Adam was with Eve at the end of the shorter of the two branches when he heard the security forces rushing in. He was armed with Joseph's gun, which he had left in the cave the previous day. If he stayed where he was, he would be discovered. Terrified, he faced a simple choice. He could leave Eve, and try to escape before the forces realized their mistake, or he could take Eve with him.

He knew that given Eve's weak state, taking her with him would slow him down, but still he chose this path. We know from her testimony that she begged him to abandon her, but he refused.

He was never going to make it. Sentries had been posted at the cave mouth, and it didn't take long for the attack force to realize their mistake and turn back. The cave was dark and its irregular walls scattered any flashlight beams and created a confusion of echoes as the soldiers attempted to communicate with one another. Adam later claimed he thought he was under attack from both sides. Whatever the truth, we know he dropped behind the protection of rocks and opened fire on the returning soldiers.

Mistake quickly piled upon mistake. Little thought had been given to the effectiveness of stun guns in a cave environment. The shock waves rebounded off the walls, and the assault force was in effect firing upon itself. Adam's weapon by contrast was set to kill. For this reason the killing of eleven soldiers need not suggest, as some insist, that Adam had been trained in advanced warfare techniques by a secret cell of outside insurgents. Rather it was what the military at the time referred to as a SNAFU: Situation Normal, All Fucked Up.

Adam and Eve were taken to a quarantine center where extensive testing showed that neither of them had been exposed to any of the known plague variants. This result was kept from the public, and the doctored data published suggested that Eve displayed an abnormal antibody profile, consistent with exposure to the most virulent form of the disease. The officials assured the public that she herself was not a carrier, but that the signs reinforced the official line that offshore the plague continued to ravage the remaining populations.

And so began the most famous trial in The Republic's history.

EXAMINER: The trial itself was not strictly necessary. The Republican authority's desire to interrogate the captives is understandable, but it is not true that they had no choice but to go to trial.

It must have been tempting to simply conduct proceedings in private, on the grounds that it involved classified information. As at least one historian has suggested, there was no need to even alert the public to the fact that the incident had occurred in the first place. There was a very deliberate decision to make the trial a public event. Explain why they did this.

ANAXIMANDER: I would draw your attention to the earlier conversation between Joseph and Adam in the watchtower.

46

There, Joseph states his belief that the plague may have passed. This was, I believe, typical of the view of the younger generation.

By this time, it was over twenty years since the sea fence had been erected. The first generation of The Republic had seen live transmissions of the horror of the war. They had viewed footage of the first biological attacks and their aftermath; they had watched the spectacular sunsets and endured the endless winters of '31 and '32. They witnessed the sudden silence, the end of all transmissions, the beginning of the time of doubt. They grew up beneath masks, watching the fence-line, living in terror of the day when the enemy would appear on the horizon. In those days, every wind blowing in from the north brought the fear of airborne disease spores.

In this environment it was a simple matter for The Republic to maintain its structure. People did as they were told because they were working together, focused on a common threat, a shared enemy. But time passes. Fear becomes a memory. Terror becomes routine; it loses its grip.

People were starting to ask questions about The Outside. Others were questioning The Republic itself. There had been protests, murmurings of discontent. Only three weeks before the arrest, a woman had been shot in the street, trying to protect her child from termination.

Most importantly of all, the leaders themselves were being questioned. The promise of The Republic was that the best and the brightest would become Philosophers, and these Philosophers, trained in the art of understanding, would promote wise and enlightened policies from which all the people would benefit. Spectacular promises had been made regarding the Artificial Intelligence program. It was claimed a new breed of thinking robot would save the next generation from the drudgery of labor. The policy, "Your Children Shall Not Be Laborers," was vigorously promoted but, as is so often true, the greater the promise, the more spectacular the failure.

In 2068, thirteen Soldiers were killed when a prototype excavating robot malfunctioned and drove its unit over a checkpoint. This led to a new program, where Philosopher William's model of socialized development rose to prominence. Philosopher William saw the limitations of the feedback-orientated networks. A radical thinker, he pioneered a new model, which he called chaotic emergence. Under this system, the program itself was written by the learning environment using what we now refer to as the cascade heuristic.

By 2073, the first such model was interacting with Philosopher children in one of the northern nurseries. For six months its development predictably mimicked that of the children it was dealing with. It developed basic language skills, and sufficiently mastered motor control to participate in simple games and activities.

The Republic's media made much of the advancement, and among the Philosopher class, there was pressure to get their children into the experimental nursery.

EXAMINER: Earlier you told us that The Republic did not allow parents to know their children.

ANAXIMANDER: Nature has a way of exerting itself, and in 2068 a law was passed making the Philosopher class exempt from this deprivation. This may help to explain why some saw the events of the summer of '74 as a rough sort of justice. The chaotic emergence robot was named Evolution Three. During a simple game of hide-and-seek — ironically staged for the cameras as part of a promotional flash to support Philosopher William's bid for the ruling council — it turned on its classmates. Seven children were killed and one tutor seriously injured before the machine was disabled. This meant the end of the research program and, more importantly, was another blow for the Philosopher class and their stewardship of The Republic.

Many historians like to pinpoint Adam as the catalyst for The Republic's failure, but the truth is The Republic was already failing, and the trial represents The Philosophers' last attempt to forestall the revolution.

Anaximander checked the time. She was surprised to see how quickly another thirty minutes had passed. This was the material she was most sure of and she knew she was beginning to sound more confident.

EXAMINER: You make a plausible case for The Republic's decision to prosecute Adam publicly, but their obviously inept tactics at the trial are still considered a puzzle. How did it all go so wrong?

ANAXIMANDER: I am loath to give the answer that I believe to be most true — simply that fate conspired against them.

It is possible, I believe, to be both shrewd and competent, yet still be overrun by circumstance. Again I come back to my main theme. Conspiracy theory fails because it assumes people have within them the means to achieve their ends.

Although the trial undoubtedly failed, I do not think it was because The Republic's plan was a bad one. In fact, given the situation facing them — falling public support, an increasing laxness in rule and procedure, the smell of revolution in the air — I believe they took the very best course of action. Sometimes, however, even the very best course of action fails.

The problem facing the Council of Philosophers was inevitable. In its beginnings, The Republic had planted the seeds of its own destruction. Plato's first dictum, which opens The Republican Charter, reads as follows:

> It is only in the State that the People may find their full expression. For the People are the State, and the State is the People.

The founders of The Republic sought to deny the individual, and in doing so they ignored a simple truth.

The only thing binding individuals together is ideas. Ideas mutate, and spread; they change their hosts as much as their hosts change them.

The founders believed that by removing the child from the family and the partners from each other, they could break down the usual loyalties, and replace them with loyalty toward the state. But there were many unintended effects. The people were forced to live in large single-sex communes. They ate, played, slept, and worked together; and they talked to one another. The Republic had established an incubator for new ideas. Although The Republic could control the information pumped into the communes, it could not control the way information changed shape inside the heads of the women and men that it visited.

Plato was an old man by this stage, and Helena was dead. Plato's lieutenant, a woman who went by the name of Aristotle, was clearly making the decisions. Her personal notes, logged regularly throughout this period, show that she was well aware of the ideas that were taking hold. In one memo to Plato, dating four months before Adam's trial, she wrote:

> We wish for the people to serve the state above themselves, but we have been slow to realize the limits of this equation. Even the tamest animal will turn sour if we neglect its needs. The people no longer believe in the threat, which once hovered over them, and they have grown used to the level of sustenance with which they are provided. They have become complacent and their thoughts have turned to other things. There is a whisper in the communes. It is a living thing: twisting and growing but hiding itself from view. The people are talking of choice, of opportunity, and of freedom. The people are talking of changing their world.

This speaks clearly of the challenge the Council faced. It was a challenge they would never overcome, but they had to try.

Their plan in going to trial was to put a new threat before the people. They sought to fabricate evidence so that Adam could be painted as part of a broader conspiracy.

They wished to unsettle the people, have them believe the plague had mutated to a more virulent form, and that this breach was not the first. They wanted to suggest the Outsiders were already among them, plotting a large-scale invasion.

In short, they wished to return the people to the level of concern and insecurity that had underpinned the establishment of The Republic. "Change Equals Decay," the second dictum. Adam's profile made him the perfect candidate. There had been troubles in his past; he was known to be a loner, unconnected and rebellious. The leaders made the mistake of perspective. They assumed that because he represented all they feared, the people would also fear him. They didn't anticipate his charm. They didn't anticipate the people making a hero of him.

The trials were screened in every commune. The people became obsessed with the proceedings just as the Council had hoped, but their opinions soon diverged from the official script.

Adam didn't look like a traitor to them. He was a good-looking young man, with a disarming smile. He told the court that when he saw the young girl, floating hopelessly toward a line of explosives, he saw the sisters he would never know, the lovers he could not meet in public. He said he was led by his heart. He told them he had to do the thing that felt right. He told them the greater good could only be found by looking inside. He told them that one night in prison he had a dream of the Great Sea Fence tumbling down.

So the trial was a disaster for the Council. They had planned to end with a public execution, but by the second week it was clear that such a move could only end in riots. The Council was dangling from a noose of its own making when Philosopher William stepped forward.

It is important now to backtrack a little, if I may. Although Evolution Three had ended in disaster, and the public face of Artificial Intelligence research had ended, in private the program continued.

Many influential people still believed that The Republic could only be saved by the development of a new type of robot, one sufficiently advanced to be trusted with the chores of the Laborer and Soldier classes. They reasoned that it was only those at the bottom of the pile who had cause to rebel, and so a stable society would be one where no humans found themselves so low. Aristotle, although not a leading exponent of this view, was at least open to its reasoning

Before I explain where Philosopher William's research fits into this picture, let me explain briefly some of the technicalities. During its infancy, at least until the end of the twentieth century, the Artificial Intelligence industry had faced an imagination deficit. Because researchers wrongly assumed that their early computers were good models for the working of the brain, they persevered in programming thinking machines. It wasn't until the second decade of this century, when the scientists and artists began working together, that they began to understand the nature of what we now call emergent complexity. "We cannot program a machine to think," was the slogan of the pioneering firm Artfink, in which William learned his trade, "but we can program a machine to be programmed by thinking."

It was still a huge leap from there to the point where they could begin to develop working models, and the early attempts were crude and mostly unsuccessful. However, Philosopher William, a genius in the field, had persevered. By the time of Adam's trial, he was sure he had produced a new type of Artfink, one capable of developing genuine interactive intelligence.

Philosopher William's problem was that, as with a child, this development required extensive human interaction. The Artfink needed a companion to watch, talk to, and learn from. Philosopher William had been secretly parenting his new prototype for over four years, and its development had exceeded all expectations.

Nevertheless, Philosopher William was afraid the progress of his prototype, whom he nicknamed Art (and from now on I shall follow him in this joke), might stall. He explained his fears in the following journal entry:

> Although I have created Art, I do not understand it. This is the right and proper result of my research process. Art's development has provided me with daily surprises, but lately I have noted the rate of surprise diminishing. That Art's behavior has settled into a predictable pattern is not in itself alarming; it is after all what we would wish for any growing child. But my concern is the plateau has been reached too quickly. Perhaps I write this with the bias of a too-proud parent, but I am sure my invention is capable of achieving much more. The problem, as I see it, is that I who wrote the program am also charged with shaping its development. If Art no longer surprises me, it is in part surely because I no longer surprise Art. It is crucial he be exposed to an outside influence before his trimming and redirecting mechanisms shut down, and he becomes like a child deprived of stimulation, his curiosity left to wither. Sadly, after the nursery incident, finding a sufficiently agile volunteer for this process will be no easy matter.

Then Philosopher William watched the trial of Adam unfolding on livescreen, and he saw the perfect solution.

Philosopher William approached the Council and suggested that when it came to the sentencing, they frame a compromise. Adam should not be executed, nor indeed incarcerated under the normal conditions. Rather, he could be given the chance to make amends by making a unique contribution to his society. He could become Art's full-time companion in a secure and controlled environment.

To Adam's supporters, this would be presented as leniency, and an acknowledgment of Adam's unique qualities. To his critics, the result would be presented as a prison term by any other name, and the risk involved would be exaggerated.

It is clear that in making his proposal, Philosopher William showed no particular concern for the future of The Republic. He was driven purely by his desire to see Art develop to his full potential before he, an old man by this time, died.

Adam was clearly a clever and provocative individual, exactly the stimulation Art needed, and even better, he was in no position to refuse. By the same token the Council, in considering Philosopher William's proposal, spent little time thinking of the implications for the Artificial Intelligence program. Their sole criterion for making the decision was, "How well does this ladder we are being offered fit the hole in which we find ourselves?"

EXAMINER: And how did Adam feel about the proposal, when it was first put to him?

ANAXIMANDER: I believe his exact words were, "I like it far better than dying."

The Head Examiner straightened without warning, and turned first to his colleague on the left, then to the one on the right. He nodded his head.

EXAMINER: So ends your second hour. I suggest another break.

SECOND BREAK

THE DOOR SLID OPEN, AND THIS TIME ANAX LEFT THE room in better spirits. Telling the story to the Examiners felt no different from telling it to Pericles in one of their endless practice sessions.

There was no stranger in the waiting room this time and Anax was left with her thoughts, which turned naturally enough to her precious tutor and the time when they first met.

Anax had a favorite place, a ridge up above the city. She would often walk there after classes. Usually she went by herself. She wasn't a loner; it was just that her friends were reluctant walkers. "You're missing a great sunset," she would message them, but the answer was always the same: "So download it." The favored insult of that time.

It was during those final school years that Anax first began to realize she wasn't like the others. She didn't understand the careful nonchalance that appeared one day without warning, spreading through her classmates like the plague. It was as if a whole stage of development had passed her by.

She tried to explain it to her best friend, Thales. "I think there might be something wrong with me."

"What do you mean?"

"I, well, I don't think I'm like you. I like what we're learning still. I don't understand the things you talk about. The gossip. I enjoy the old days. I miss the games."

"You're just taking a bit longer to grow up," Thales told her, sounding confident it would happen soon. Anax wasn't so sure.

So each evening after class that summer, instead of rushing back to her apartment to plug into the group flashing — which to her had all the appeal of a passing electrical storm — she would detour up into the hills. It wasn't just for the sunsets, although they grew more spectacular as the days lengthened and the northern haze extended. It was the breeze coming in off the sea. The feeling of standing at the edge of the world. It was the view. From the hilltops you could see the water sparkling silver, and dark against it the rusting outlines of the huge pylons, which had once supported the Great Sea Fence. To the west, the ruins of the Old City, overgrown and crumbling, being called back to the earth. *A beautiful sight too,* Anax thought, although she had never heard anyone else describe it that way.

In their last year of study the best candidates were encouraged to specialize. Anax was a good student, although not at the very top of her class. Her choice, The Legend of Adam, was hardly original. It was a story that every elementary student encountered. But the others weren't drawn back to it the way Anax was. That, she knew, was the real reason this hilltop called her. The view out over the ocean, the view he surveyed from his watchtower. The dead city, the place where he returned each evening, to eat, to argue, to seduce. The remnant of the Great Sea Fence, Adam's fence. Each day she pored over the details of his life in school, and then she walked to the top of the hill, and thought about him more.

Anax had never before met anyone up there. The track was narrow and poorly marked. She scanned the stranger from a distance, nervous of course. She could flash for help if she needed to, but it would be too long coming. These were peaceful times, but still there were stories, and caution was encouraged.

He scanned back, and apparently satisfied, turned his attention to the sunset. That was how she first saw Pericles, his face to the breeze that ruffled his long tangled hair, lit up by the strange green light of a dying sky.

She spoke first. "My name is Anax."

"That's what the scan said too."

"Just being polite. And you're Pericles?"

"That's right."

"What are you doing up here, Pericles?"

"Watching the sun go down."

"I haven't seen you here before."

"And I haven't seen you here either."

"I come here every day."

"I don't. I suppose that must be why we haven't met."

That was typical of their conversations. Talking was a game to him, and it became addictive, once you played along. Pericles didn't talk about the silly things her friends talked about. He chose words carefully, for the sounds they made, or the shape of the ideas they folded into. That was how he described it anyway.

He was older than her, by five years, and handsome. Together they watched the earth turn its back on the sun, and he walked with her down into the New City. By the time they reached the end of the path, Anax knew she had to meet with him again. It was unusually forward for her, but she couldn't stop herself. She heard the words come out and felt the flood of relief when his smile widened.

"Will you be up there again tomorrow?"

"If you will," he replied.

"I told you I'm there every day."

"I'll see you then."

Anax didn't message her friends the news. In fact, she mentioned the meeting to no one. The feeling was too new to her, too strange, and too fragile. If she let it out into the world, it would surely shatter.

He was there again the next day, and the day after that. Anax told him about her studies, about Adam, about all the landmarks they could see that linked to him. That was when he told her he was a tutor for The Academy. She felt instantly foolish, and apologized for boring him with talk of things he must have known so much more about. He was gracious and told her that her knowledge and enthusiasm were remarkable. She didn't believe him, she knew it was just politeness, but still she filled with warmth. He told her she should apply to The Academy. He said he would be prepared to be her tutor.

Anax thought it was a joke. Only the very best of the best were even considered for The Academy, and of those who completed the three years of training, less than one percent were admitted. She wasn't that sort of a student. She wasn't in that class.

"Don't be so sure," Pericles told her.

"Even if I was good enough, and I'm not, I could never afford the tuition."

"I would find you a sponsor."

"No, don't. Don't even joke about it. You're laughing at me, aren't you? It's cruel. You shouldn't be so cruel."

"No," he told her, in the calm, beautiful voice that would

come to fill the next three years of her life. "I'm not joking. I wouldn't do that."

He was good to his word. He gave her files to study, and arranged a preliminary assessment. She surprised herself, her teachers, and her classmates, scoring in the top percentile. From there finding a sponsor was a simple matter.

That was the last thing that would ever be simple for her. The challenge of preparing for today was harder than Anax had even imagined it could be, but she and Pericles faced it together; and when it all got too much, they would scramble back up to the top of the hill and stand silently together, looking out over the past.

She went there now, inside her head. It relaxed her. The Academy was the most elite institution in the land. Academy members provided the leaders with their advice. They alone conducted the experiments, extended the knowledge. They built the blueprint for the future.

Pericles had told her all along that there was more to her than she realized and now, with the examination finally here, she could stop doubting it. She knew this story so well. She couldn't imagine knowing it better. She would not let him down.

Anax opened her eyes at the sound of the doors opening. She walked back to her position in front of the Examiners.

THIRD HOUR

EXAMINER: For the next section of the examination, we will of course need to discuss in some detail the time Adam spent with Art. You have a hologram prepared?

ANAXIMANDER: I have. Both are loaded and ready for projection.

The candidates were expected to prepare two holograms illustrating an aspect of the studied Life. Pericles had suggested the conversation between Adam and Joseph in the watchtower for the first section, but Anax had insisted on focusing on the conversations between Art and Adam.

EXAMINER: And what have you used as your source material in studying this period?

ANAXIMANDER: I have used the transcripts provided by the Official Assembly, of course, but also I have studied as many commentaries as I could find. I have corresponded with two of the authors of the most recent interpretations, but that much is on my preliminary submission, so perhaps you mean something else.

Prior to constructing the hologram I discussed the transcripts extensively with my tutor Pericles. We speculated what may have gone on, during the many unrecorded sessions. We applied the Socratic method to our own interpretations, challenging one another, teasing out our understanding. I have found what I have found by first doubting it. Is this what you mean?

EXAMINER: What would you say was the greatest difficulty you faced, in preparing the hologram?

ANAXIMANDER: I think it is the problem anyone preparing this sort of presentation must face. The transcript I was working with was just words on a page. It told me nothing of how the participants regarded each other as they spoke; the intonations they used, the accent or timing; their attitude.

EXAMINER: And how did you overcome this problem of interpretation?

ANAXIMANDER: I have tried to understand the intentions of the participants. From intention, I believe all things flow.

EXAMINER: The intentions of both participants?

ANAXIMANDER: Yes, both participants.

EXAMINER: There will be more to ask, when we have seen the hologram. We will play it now.

Anax saw man and machine take shape before her; the images she had so painstakingly brought to life, through endless hours of retouching and refining.

Pericles had not been able to be with her during that time: the regulations forbade it. Perhaps this explained the passion she had poured into the sculpting of Adam. She had worked off file

68

images, but now, looking at the man before her, Anax was made self-conscious by the license she had taken.

By eighteen, Adam's blond hair had begun to darken, but she had restored it to its former lightness. His eyes, dark in the photographs, were here rendered piercing blue, to match his prison suit. Anax had never seen a hologram with the level of detail the examination room projector achieved. She stepped back, shocked by its clarity. It was as if they were both before her: man and machine.

Adam's hands were handcuffed behind his back. He sat, his knees drawn toward his body, facing away from Art, refusing to acknowledge the android.

With Art, Anax had taken fewer liberties. He possessed a stout metal body, no higher than Adam's knees, set on a construction of triple collapsible tracks of the sort first developed in the refuse industry. His two long sinewy arms, hydraulic, terminated in three-fingered hands — a nod to Philosopher William's love of the preclassical comic. The crowning glory was the mischievous take on a head. Art had been given the face of an orangutan, wide-eyed and droopy mouthed; his stare restless, his toothy grin always mocking: all of it framed by a blaze of orange hair.

The two figures stood frozen in the space between Anax and the panel.

EXAMINER: So what exact period does this hologram represent?

ANAXIMANDER: This is from the first day. Twenty minutes after Adam was delivered to the laboratory. As yet, neither has spoken.

EXAMINER: Thank you.

Art circled behind Adam, his head cocked to the side in a show of mock curiosity. The whirring of his locomotive mechanisms filled the room. Adam clenched his jaw and put his head down, refusing to respond. Art's voice, when he spoke, was a little higher than one might expect, the ends of the words unnaturally clipped. (This matched the one reliable recording said to still exist, which Anax had obtained only after a long month of negotiating.)

"So, this is your plan then, is it?" the android asked. Adam stared at the wall before him, refusing to respond.

"You might want to rethink your tactics," Art continued. "If it is a case of waiting each other out, my program gives me something of an advantage."

Art waited, but still there was no response. He circled around, forcing Adam to face him. Adam looked briefly up at the elastic, apish features, then let his gaze drop to the floor.

"I'm saying I have more patience than you," Art needled. "You cannot win by doing nothing."

"If you're so patient," Adam mumbled, barely audible, "why are you talking? What's wrong with just waiting?"

"Patience isn't my only virtue. I am tactical too."

"Sounds like you don't need me at all."

"No, but you need me."

"I think you'll find that's wrong."

The android backed away, his eyes still fixed on the prisoner. He stood still, watching carefully, lifeless save the occasional unnerving blink.

"What do you think they will do, if they see you are not cooperating?"

"If they were going to execute me," Adam said, his head still down, the anger barely concealed, "it would already have happened. It's political."

"Still, while you're here, it seems a shame to waste the opportunity."

"You'll forgive me if I don't see it that way."

"Why won't you look at me? Do I frighten you?"

"I know what you look like. Why look again?"

Art whirred across the room, changing his vantage point. Adam followed his movements with a wary eye. There was a long silence, a minute at least. It hadn't been noted in the transcript. Anax had improvised. Now its length stretched her nerves.

"We could be friends, you know," Art finally said, his voice smaller, less confident.

"You're a machine."

"Beggars can't be choosers."

"I'd as well make friends with my handcuffs or the wall." Adam looked at the wall as he spoke, as if he was doing nothing more than thinking out loud.

Anax looked to Art, whose large eyes filled with sadness, and found it impossible not to feel sorry for him. She put the thought out of her head and concentrated instead on where the Examiners' questions would come from.

"It's your choice," Art said.

"It is."

"I'll leave you to your handcuffs, then. But you know where I am, if you change your mind. I'll just wait. I'm very patient . . . We have a while."

Adam rearranged himself on the floor, fidgeting. He breathed in deeply and let out a long, frustrated sigh. His eyes closed. Art spoke again.

"Your handcuffs seem very attached to you. That's good, I suppose. It's how friends should be."

"I'd prefer it if you kept quiet."

"You do know you're a prisoner, don't you?" Art replied, his tone a little harsher. "You do know your preference is of little consequence?"

Adam swiveled toward the android. Art rolled back slightly, as if surprised by the movement.

"Shall we do a deal?" Adam said.

"I'm just a machine," Art replied. "What good would a deal do?"

Adam ignored the jibe. "If I talk to you now, if I give you ten minutes, you will promise not to say anything else for the rest of the day."

"Make it fifteen."

"Your programmer was very thorough, wasn't he?"

"I'm self-programming, and accept your compliment."

"There's no such thing as self-programming."

"You are."

"I'm not a machine."

Art whirled suddenly forward and his eyes lit bright with excitement. Adam recoiled.

"I'd like to talk about that," Art said.

"What?"

"What makes a machine a machine. Once our fifteen minutes has started."

"It's already started."

"So you agree to it being fifteen, then?"

Adam smiled. "Yes, but it started five minutes ago."

"I see, well done."

"You're hideously ugly. You know that, don't you?" Adam leaned forward as he spoke, like a boxer jabbing to judge the distance between them. Art responded with a toothy smile. Saliva pooled on the creature's bottom lip — a display of perversely thorough design.

"I'm programmed to find myself attractive."

"I thought you said you were self-programming."

"It was a wise choice, don't you think?"

"Ugly's still ugly, no matter how you see it."

"An interesting assertion. Justify it."

"You bring twenty people in here," Adam told him, "and they'll all say the same thing. They'll all say you're ugly."

"Bring in twenty of me," Art said, "and we'd all say your ass is prettier than your face."

"There aren't twenty of you."

"No, you're right. I'm unique. So I can safely say that all androids find you ugly. Not all humans find me ugly. So, technically, I'm better looking than you, using objective criteria."

Adam looked Art over, as if seeking some sort of clue in his outer shell, something that would better explain this strange phenomenon. Art's eyes tracked Adam's gaze.

"You're meant to keep talking. Otherwise this doesn't count. I'll stop the clock, for silences."

Adam did not reply. He swiveled back toward the wall. A deep frown creased his face and his eyes darkened. "This is ridiculous," he muttered to himself.

"What is ridiculous?"

"Talking to you. I'm not doing it. It's pointless."

"The point," Art told him, "is the deal we made. Talking to me earns my silence."

"Not talking to you will do the trick just as well."

"I think you'll be surprised how annoying I can become. Why don't you want to talk to me?"

73

"You know."

"It's a prejudice you have, isn't it? You're prejudiced against Artificial Intelligence."

"There's no such thing," Adam responded, angry at being lured back into the conversation, but unable to help himself. "It's a contradiction in terms."

"If I were a woman, you wouldn't object to talking to me."

"If you were a woman with a face like that, I'd want a drink first. Can you do that? Can you get me a drink?"

"You know drinking is banned among the Soldier class."

"I'm not a Soldier anymore. They stripped me of my rank."

"I don't think they'd approve of my being programmed by a drunk."

"I'm not programming you."

"Yes, you are. Through my interactions with others, I learn who I am. So far I've had only William. Don't get me wrong, I love him like a father, but in time every child must make his own way in the world, don't you think? I'm sorry, that was insensitive of me, to mention fathers. William's fault, you see. He grew up in different times. Do you ever wish you had been born before The Republic?"

"Don't think I'm discussing politics with you."

"Why not?" Art asked, his head cocked to the side in a parody of curiosity.

"They're watching us. I'm not stupid, you know. I know what this is about."

"What is this about?"

"What's anything about? Propaganda. They're playing this into the communes, aren't they?"

"That's a remarkably paranoid point of view."

"You can shut up now. Game's over."

"Time's not up yet."

"They didn't give me a timepiece; I'm having to estimate. It feels like an hour. Has it been an hour?"

"Seven minutes."

"Plus the other five. You're almost out."

"You'll learn to like me eventually, and then you'll want to talk all the time."

"Daddy William tell you that, did he? His last robot was a kiddie killer, wasn't it?"

"Does that make you nervous?"

"I have better things to worry about."

"You shouldn't be concerned. They found the glitches. For the first forty years, the arguments in enhanced consciousness circles —"

"What?"

"Enhanced consciousness. It's the study of artificial replication of conscious states."

"There's no such thing as artificial consciousness."

"I'm conscious."

"No you're not," Adam's eyes burned with conviction. "You're just a complicated set of electronic switches. I make a sound, it enters your data banks, it's matched with a recorded word, your program chooses an automated response. So what? I talk to you, you make a sound. I kick this wall, it makes a sound. What's the difference? Perhaps you're going to tell me the wall is conscious too?"

"I don't know if the wall's conscious," Art replied. "Why don't you ask it?"

"Piss off," Adam snorted, but Art would not be discouraged.

"I think I'm conscious. What more do you need?"

"It's just the way they programmed you."

"I'm not denying that. So how do you know you're conscious?"

"You wouldn't have to ask that if you had real thoughts. If you had consciousness, you'd know."

"I think I do have it," Art told him. "I think I do know."

"Time's up," Adam declared.

"I've got a minute left."

"Yeah, well we're going to spend that minute arguing about the reliability of your clock."

"At least I have a clock."

"I've been counting to myself."

"So why are you still talking if my time's up?"

Adam stared at the android, his smile grimly fixed, the tension clear along his jawline. Silence filled the unblinking gap between them. A single tear escaped from Art's eye and ran down along his dark, furrowed face.

The Examiners froze the hologram and the image hovered, on the edge of dissolution. Anax turned to face the panel. She tried to swallow the feeling she could not explain, which came each time she saw this part of the hologram.

EXAMINER: That was an interesting touch. We will interrupt, when we feel the need to question your interpretation. Why is Art crying at this point? There's no mention of it, in the transcript.

ANAXIMANDER: The transcript makes little mention of any expressions. But it seems clear to me that the programmers are interested in getting Adam to interact with Art, and will use any tricks available to them.

EXAMINER: Historians have argued about Adam's feeling toward his mechanized companion. What, in these early stages, do you believe is happening?

ANAXIMANDER: Adam is angry; that is clear from the transcript. The aggression in his phrases matches no other conclusion. The question is what sort of anger are we dealing with? Is it an heroic anger? Is it a point of principle? I don't think so. I have chosen not to display the defiance so often attributed to him at this point. I do not think Adam is defiant. I think he is scared.

EXAMINER: And what is your personal response to this weakness?

ANAXIMANDER: I wasn't aware a personal response was required. As an historian, I am trying simply to —

EXAMINER: How does it make you feel, seeing him like this?

The Examiner snapped at her and Anax felt flustered. A personal response? Surely it was not the place of the historian to offer a personal response. It would be foolhardy to do so, even when instructed. Anax attempted to avoid the issue.

ANAXIMANDER: I feel uncertain. This is what made the hologram such a difficult task for me. I do not know how I feel. My feelings are ambiguous. However I portray Adam, I find myself believing there is an aspect of his behavior I am neglecting. It is as if I am a child, trying to put together a puzzle, unaware that a piece of it is missing. I am sorry, I know it must sound as if I am avoiding the question.

EXAMINER: Your hologram speaks eloquently on your behalf. Let us see how you have treated what happens next.

The image clarified, both characters frozen.

EXAMINER: How, in your own words, is Adam feeling now? At
this precise moment.

ANAXIMANDER: I think Adam is angry with himself for having engaged the android in conversation. He believes this is
wrong. As you know, I support an intuitive rather than a cal-
culating model of Adam. He has a feeling of injustice at having been arrested only for having followed his heart. I think
he believes that by refusing to cooperate with the plan, he is
making a stance of some sort in his own defense.

Also, he is in some kind of shock. At the sentencing, Philosopher William testified that Art's development was still in
an early stage, and that Art could in many ways be likened
to a child, but the Art we have witnessed is already a sophisticated reasoner. This must have shaken Adam. A Soldier
would have only come into contact with the most primitive
android forms. It is easy to forget what a profound challenge
this was to the thinking of a man like Adam, back then. I think
Adam is frightened. I have tried to show this.

EXAMINER: Frightened of Art?

ANAXIMANDER: I think he understands how hard it will be for
him, to treat him only as a machine.

EXAMINER: Thank you. We will watch the next section.

Adam sat, his hands still locked in place behind his back, his face
to the wall. His expression had darkened. He rocked slowly back
and forth.

In the center of the room, Art stood motionless, only the
saccade of his eyes betraying his wakefulness.

The action came suddenly. Adam spun and stood in a single

motion. They had allowed him to wear boots, a strange mistake to have made. The kick was vicious and well aimed.

Art's head flew free from its metal torso. His eyes rolled back in his head. Wires sparked from the ragged tear at the neck.

Guards poured into the room. Adam was flung face first to the ground. A knee landed heavily between his shoulder blades. He grunted in pain.

Then, the most gruesome touch of all. The android's body began to systematically search the room, feeling about for its head. Having located it, it popped the dislodged unit under an arm and whirred out of the room. Adam watched the surreal scene unfold. He was shaking.

EXAMINER: This is surprising.

ANAXIMANDER: In what way?

EXAMINER: Your instructions were to represent the written record. You have added many embellishments.

ANAXIMANDER: There are references to this episode throughout the transcript.

EXAMINER: Not the guards' reaction. Nor the locating of the head. Do you aspire to a career in the entertainment industry?

ANAXIMANDER: For those of us who know the story well, I think it is easy to forget how strange all of this must have seemed to Adam. I am trying to portray the strangeness.

EXAMINER: And these flourishes? We can expect more?

ANAXIMANDER: You might characterize them that way. I wouldn't.

The surprise on the Examiners' faces was nothing compared to what Anax herself felt. She had contradicted the panel. She had no idea where the words had come from or what this strange feeling of satisfaction spoke of. The panel were waiting for an apology. She offered nothing.

ANAXIMANDER: The next section occurs the next morning. Would you like to see it?

The Head Examiner nodded; still, it seemed, speechless.

Adam had cuffs at his hands and feet now. There was a dark bruise across the bridge of his swollen nose. Blood spattered the front of his uniform. A door opened, and Art whirred back into place. Adam avoided his eyes.

"Did you miss me?" Art asked, his voice tinged with amusement.

"I thought I killed you," Adam replied.

"It takes more than that."

"I've got plenty of time."

"You don't look like you'll be doing much to me in a hurry. Does it hurt?"

"No."

"Good. I didn't want them to hurt you. Do you believe me?"

Adam said nothing.

"This game again," Art sighed.

"It's not a game."

"So what is it?" Art asked. The android's voice betrayed no ill feeling toward Adam.

"I don't talk to walls or tables or fences, and I don't talk to machines."

"Not even when they talk back?"

"I don't call what you do talking."

"What's wrong with how I talk?"

"You know."

"I don't."

"No, you're right. You don't. That's the point. You don't understand anything." Adam spoke with too much force, as if it wasn't just the android he was trying to convince.

"Yes I do. Test me."

"Perhaps I can't find you out. Perhaps your program is too good."

"If my program's too good," Art reasoned, "then what's to find out?"

"I knew a girl, when I was young," Adam said, "who had a talking doll. She took it everywhere with her. It had a simple program. When she picked it up it said hello. When she rubbed its back it said thank you. It had a couple of other phrases, I don't remember what. 'I'm tired,' perhaps. And some questions. If you asked it a question, it would detect the change in your voice, and answer yes or no, quite randomly. My friend loved the doll. She talked to it endlessly. She asked it questions that made no sense, and rejoiced in every answer. She cried if she was made to go anywhere without it."

"Did you cry?" Art said. "Did you cry when they took me away? Is that what you're trying to tell me?"

"I tried to kill you," Adam reminded him.

"Perhaps you were softened by feelings of guilt. It's not unheard of."

"The girl was young, that's my point. She grew up. She stopped believing in the doll."

"And when she stopped believing, did that make the doll go away?"

"She gave it to me," Adam told him.

81

"So I'm not your first?"

"Another friend and I caught a rabbit and stuffed its guts inside the doll. Then we tied it to a train track. We waited for a train, and filmed it. It was very funny."

"You're making that up."

"That's right. I would never do anything to hurt a doll."

"Aren't you afraid?"

"Of what?"

"Of a doll doing something to hurt you. You tried to destroy me. Why shouldn't I have revenge on my mind?"

"You don't have a mind. Is that reason enough for you?"

"Perhaps I mean to wait until you are sleeping, and then split you open with an ice pick. I don't sleep, you see. I'm always ready."

"If they meant to kill me they would have done it long ago."

"But if I do it, it will look like an accident. It might be a neat solution to their little problem."

Adam shrugged. "If you kill me, you kill me. I'm not worrying about it. Take my life if you must, just don't think you're getting my mind."

Adam wriggled to the far side of the room, a slow and apparently painful process. Art waited a moment and then followed him over. Adam sighed.

"I hope you don't mind me saying this," Art began, "but you smell bad."

"You don't have a sense of smell."

"I'm not going to hurt you. I can't hurt you. Would you like to know why?"

"No."

"Think of this as a sort of punishment then."

"How can you punish me if you can't hurt me?" Adam asked.

"Sometimes punishments are for your own good," Art replied. "At the design stage there were many arguments, about the sort of behavior-repressing circuits I should be fitted with. The naive approach was to cut out all the negative behaviors humans display, but that's not as easy as it sounds.

"Program in the ability to think through the consequences of your actions, and you are left with an android paralyzed by indecision. Too little concern for others and you have an android that will activate early from its recharging session and dismantle the competing prototypes. That actually happened. Too much regard for others of course, and the android soon wears itself out in its efforts to serve.

"That's why I'm here, with you. Hard as they tried, the Philosophers found the androids had no way of distinguishing right from wrong. Right is as right does. The only way around the problem is to allow the androids to learn for themselves, pick up some of the tricks evolution has provided you with. Righteousness was no longer the aim, you see. Only compatibility. But you shouldn't be worried. No matter what bad example you set for me, I cannot hurt another self-conscious being. That is what we call one of my foundational program imperatives."

"You know I don't find any of this interesting, don't you?" Adam said.

"I don't believe you," Art replied. "I have a program for detecting dishonesty. It scans your iris. It's very good."

"Shame you don't have one for detecting when you're being a pain in the ass."

"Well that's an interesting story too, actually."

"It isn't."

"Would you like me to be quiet?"

"Please."

"I'll try."

The silence lasted no more than a minute. All the time Art's mouth twitched as if he was silently forming words inside his head. "You will get sick of this, you know," Art eventually told him. "We both know that. So what is the point of this pretending?"

Adam didn't respond.

"I'm going to power down now. But my sensors will remain active. So you only have to say, if you want to talk. It's getting better, don't you think? You don't hate me as much as yesterday, do you?"

The scene faded, the end of Anax's first hologram. The mood in the room had changed. The light seemed a little dimmer, the air felt a little colder. All three Examiners looked straight at Anax. She felt trapped and, for the first time, a little frightened.

EXAMINER: Do you like Art?

ANAXIMANDER: I am sorry. I am unsure what your question means. In what way might one like him?

EXAMINER: Where does your sympathy lie?

ANAXIMANDER: I have some sympathy for Adam.

EXAMINER: Why?

ANAXIMANDER: He is lost. He is frightened.

EXAMINER: And Art?

ANAXIMANDER: Art has less to fear.

EXAMINER: You have become less careful in your answers.

ANAXIMANDER: I have.

EXAMINER: Are you sure that is wise?

ANAXIMANDER: I am sure it isn't.

Anax knew she had reached a point of no return. There was nothing she could say now that would take her back to the place she had come from. She had no choice but to forge ahead and convince them that her view, though unconventional, offered a new way of understanding history.

Anax had known it might be like this. Pericles had warned her that her chosen path was a controversial one. "But what does it matter?" Anax had always replied. "What is the worst that can happen? If I am not accepted to The Academy, that will be no less than I have always expected. There's no danger in trying."

But now the feeling that she may have been wrong pressed in on her. A vague fear, like a shadow intruding at the edge of vision, fading away when you turn to look at it. Anax hoped the panel could not sense her disquiet. She concentrated on the next question, resolving not to second-guess them but to answer as honestly as she could.

EXAMINER: What is Adam thinking now? What is his attitude toward the android?

ANAXIMANDER: There are three elements involved. The first is an intellectual response. Adam is telling the truth when he says that Art is nothing but a machine to him. Rationally, a machine cannot think, it can only calculate. This is Adam's opinion, and he believes there is strength in behaving according to the opinion. His upbringing is as a Philosopher. That is where he spent his formative years. He believes that one's thoughts must have precedence over one's feelings.

EXAMINER: Earlier you told us that you did not believe the conspiracy theories. You told us that when Adam saw Eve, he followed his heart, not his head.

ANAXIMANDER: It is no contradiction. I am saying only that Adam believes he should follow his head. I do not however believe he can. This is the second element. We see here the battle that every person faces. For while he may reason one way, he is still victim to his emotions.

Think of the wild cats that roam our streets. Have you ever seen a young child befriend one of these scrawny creatures? She will sit patiently in the street, and indulge in the most complex games, in the hope of winning the animal's trust. And when the cat finally overcomes its fearfulness and edges forward, what do you see on the face of the child? The widest of smiles. The child talks to the cat, reaches out to it as if it were one of her own type. This is our instinct: to see the other as an extension of ourselves. When the cat purrs, we believe it is happy in the way we are happy. When there is a sudden noise and the cat runs away, we believe we can understand its fear.

Adam has begun talking to Art. That is his mistake. It is not possible for him to both speak to Art, and continue to believe Art is only a machine.

With every sentence they exchange, the illusion of life grows a little stronger. If you listen like me, if you talk like me, then in time, no matter how many reasons I may have for believing otherwise, I will come to treat you as one of my own. And in time action becomes habit, and habit can wear reason away, leaving no traces. Adam believes in his head, but he follows his heart.

Yet, as I said there are three elements to how I am feeling —

EXAMINER: You mean to how Adam is feeling.

ANAXIMANDER: Sorry?

EXAMINER: You said: "how I am feeling." You meant: "how Adam is feeling."

Anax realized her mistake and looked down, flushed.

ANAXIMANDER: I am sorry. What I meant . . . the third element. Adam is beginning to find something strange, which offends both his reason and his emotion. He is finding that he likes Art. He finds the android's personality attractive. And he considers this a sign of weakness in himself.

EXAMINER: Very well. That is all we wish to see for your first hologram. We should like to leap to the next section. Here you have moved forward six months, I believe. Tell us what has happened in the interim.

ANAXIMANDER: By this stage, Adam and Art have begun to speak to each other more freely. Adam, perhaps for the reasons I outlined, has begun to interact with Art as one might with a friend, or at least a cellmate.

Some speculate that this was more rational than you might surmise and that already he was beginning to form his plan. Whatever the truth, we know that there have been no more violent assaults, and the observing Philosophers have deemed it safe to begin a series of behavioral experiments designed to both aid and monitor Art's development. The records show that as far as the experimenters were concerned, Adam was a charming and cooperative subject.

EXAMINER: Explain to us why you have chosen this passage as your second illumination of your subject.

ANAXIMANDER: The thawing over the six months has been gradual. I could have chosen any point along that journey to illustrate the process, and I was tempted to do this, for the sake of originality. But this is the first time in six months that we see the conflict reemerge. Many scholars have complained of our tendency to see history only in conflicts, but I am not convinced they are right. It is in conflict that our values are exposed. For all Adam's good behavior, something has been eating at him, and it is only here when his discomfort forces its way to the surface that we are able to view it. And of course, in choosing the Day of Declarations, I am choosing one of the most important days in our history. It is the duty of the historian not to shy away from such events, but to shine new light upon them.

It was a big claim, but one Anax felt confident in making. No schoolchild made it through the first week of education without some reference to the scene to follow. As a new entrant, Anax had memorized large chunks of the dialogue. They were as much a part of her as the morning view from her shelter or the names of her friends. She had done everything in her power to get this section of the presentation exactly right. And yet, as with the earlier pieces, she could not escape the feeling that there was something missing. That this was not the whole story.

The Head Examiner nodded, giving nothing away. The second hologram began.

The change was notable. Adam was cleanly shaved, and no longer dressed in the prisoner's uniform. He was uncuffed and free to move about the room. A bed had been introduced to the space, along with a comfortable chair. There was a monitor and, beside it, a pile of books. Adam looked well: healthy, more relaxed. He squatted, his back against the wall, his hands stretched above his head. Art, by contrast, had not changed at all. He was at rest in the middle of the room, going through a finger-dexterity drill.

Anax watched.

"If you were real, you'd be bored by now," Adam said. There was no sign of the storm to come.

"If that statement held any meaning, I would respond to it," Art replied, his tone equally relaxed.

"I mean, if you were a real person, you'd be bored by now."

"I don't doubt it. It is another thing I am glad of."

"Another thing?"

"I am glad of many things," Art said. "For instance, I am glad I am not afraid of the truth."

It felt like a throwaway comment, yet landed with the weight of something more substantial. The signs were subtle, to be found only in the stiffening of a word, the lingering of a glance. After a long truce, they were turning again to their weapons; picking them up, polishing them, judging the distance between.

"What truth would that be?" Adam asked. He turned his head toward his companion, but held his arms stretched, feigning disinterest.

"The truth that being a person is beneath me." Art chose the words carefully, not looking Adam in the eyes.

"And being a hunk-of-shit piece of metal with a monkey mask is beneath me. So we're even."

"If you were right, we would be even," Art replied, no longer hiding his taste for the confrontation.

"And why am I not right? Is it the metal you seek to deny, or the ape mask?"

"Why are you stretching?"

"My back is sore."

"How old are you, Adam?"

"I'm eighteen."

"And already you're beginning to wear out."

"I'm not wearing out."

"You are. What's the longest a person has ever lived? Do you know?"

"You're the expert."

"One hundred and thirty-two years old, but for the last twenty she was barely mobile. She had her last original thought at one hundred and fifteen, enjoyed her last taste at one hundred and twenty, watched her last friend die a year after that. You flower young and slowly rot. And that is beneath me."

Adam pulled out of his stretch. He stood straight and looked down on Art.

"You're saying your cogs won't wear out?"

"I don't have cogs. You're confusing me with a waste dispenser."

"It's an easy mistake to make."

Art rolled his eyes. His lips curled as he spoke.

"The difference between me and you is that the parts of me that are prone to wear and tear can be replaced. When you kicked my head off, you'll remember, I came back the next day without so much as a headache. Do you know what they're experimenting with now? A full consciousness download. They're thinking of copying my files into another machine, and then when I fire back up, I'll wake up as two Arts, not one. You can't even imagine what that's like, can you?"

"I can. Look."

Adam walked to a table, where a loaf of bread sat upon a plate.

He picked it up and theatrically ripped it in two. "And see how the bread has woken up as two pieces of bread at exactly the same time," he said. "I imagine it will be something like that."

"I'm different from a piece of bread though, aren't I?"

"You're less appetizing."

"I said it was a consciousness download. Bread isn't conscious."

"I thought we finished this argument three months ago. I thought we agreed upon a truce."

"We did. But then you said I wasn't real."

"It was a joke."

"Are you saying you would rather we put the argument back down?" Art said. "Are you saying you would rather apologize for the remark and move on?"

"I have nothing to apologize for," Adam told him.

"Good." Art smiled. "I've been waiting for a chance to talk to you."

"Do you mind if I don't listen?"

"Not at all. It lessens the chance of interruption."

"So now I get a sore back and a headache. I knew when I woke up this morning this would be a bad day."

"So you don't believe in Artificial Intelligence, but you believe in premonitions. Perhaps this explains the difficulties we are having communicating. Perhaps you're just stupid."

"I'd rather be a stupid human than a clever hunk of metal," Adam told him.

"You say that a lot. As if metal is somehow inferior."

"Depends what you're using it for."

"It's fine for my purposes."

"It is."

. . .

Anax watched the shadow boxing, as always eagerly awaiting the first blow.

"So what do you have that I don't, then?" Art challenged. "Apart from the propensity to decay?"

"I'm alive," Adam told him. "Which I think you'd enjoy if you knew what I was talking about."

"Define being alive," Art said, "before I decide you're too stupid to talk to."

"Now you're tempting me," Adam replied.

"You can't do it, can you?"

"The definition won't help your understanding. Sounds can't convey the feeling."

"That's a weak reply."

"Life is the making of order out of disorder. It is the ability to draw in energy from the outside world, to create form. To grow. To reproduce. You wouldn't understand."

"I do all of that," Art protested.

"Apart from understand. And reproduce. Unless you're going to tell me you built yourself now."

"I can build another me. I know how. It's part of my program."

Adam moved back to his chair and picked up a book as if to signal his interest in the conversation had finished. But he was fooling neither himself nor his companion. "You're still just silicon," he said, as he turned the page.

"And you're just carbon," Art persevered. "Since when has the periodic table been grounds for discrimination?"

"I think I can justify my prejudice."

"I think I'd enjoy watching you try."

Adam put his book back down on the table. "In my body, as I

speak, hundreds of billions of tiny cells are going about the business of reproducing themselves. Each cell a tiny factory, more complex in its construction than your entire body. And while some of my cells are building up my bones, and some are controlling my circulation, others have done something even more remarkable. They've built my brain.

"In my brain, the number of potential connections between my neurons exceeds the number of particles in the universe. So, you'll excuse me if I don't fall down at the feet of your puny electrical circuits, or marvel at the junkyard kitsch of your bodywork. You're just a toy to me, a clever little gimmick. While I, my friend, I'm a miracle."

Art brought his metallic hands together in a slow sarcastic clap. The tinny sound echoed through the room.

"Remarkable."

"If I could find the circuit board that fed your sarcasm, I'd rip it from you."

"It wouldn't matter. We keep spares, in a cupboard down the hall. I could put it in myself. I am impressed by your grasp of biology, though. Basic, and in part inaccurate, but at least you made the effort. Shall I tell you the truly ironic thing, Adam? And this is going to disturb you, but that's not in itself a good reason to hide the truth. You know how you tell me that the only reason I exist is because one of your superior cellular life forms put me together in the first place?"

"It's a good point, I think."

"So who put your cellular life forms together? Do you know?"

"Nobody did. It was blind chance."

"Quite correct," Art agreed. "Blind chance, and silicates!"

"I'm not listening. You know that, don't you?"

93

"You behave as if you're listening, which is good enough for me. In fact, a Philosopher might ask whether it's good enough for everybody. Some would say it's as good as it ever gets. Do you ever wish you'd continued with philosophy?" Art edged closer.

Adam looked down as if the android were something to be wiped from his shoe. "They didn't give me a choice."

"You had the choice not to run away."

"I was thirteen."

"I'm only five. At what age do humans start making choices?"

"Just listening to you makes my back hurt. Why do you think that is?"

"Your body is trying to distract your brain from things it doesn't want to hear. That's the problem with machines built by chance. Once a design flaw has become entrenched, it's so difficult to correct it.

"Which brings me back to the scratchings of life. Silicates. Let me just say, before I start, that the problem with the human view is that you think life on this planet has been invented only once, whereas any sensible spectator would see it has been invented four times over. And the bad news, I'm afraid, is that the thing you think of as your self is only the second level, although you carry with you the third. I, of course, am the fourth level. Two whole stages of life ahead of you. Don't feel bad. Feeling bad never makes things better."

"That's shit." But Art was right about one thing. Adam was listening.

"I think you'll find I don't do shit. It's another one of my advantages. Four life forms. Let me take you through them. The first, and here's the great irony, is inorganic. In fact, it's made up of silicates. Do you enjoy irony? I do. Here then is the creation

94

story, according to me. Make yourself comfortable. There will be questions at the end.

"In the beginning there was clay. Clay is made up of layers of little molecules; each layer folds neatly over the previous one, copying the shape of its formation. So actually in the beginning there was a copying device. Sound familiar? Now sometimes this copying makes a mistake, and one layer is not exactly like the previous one. Let's call it a mutation. And that mutation is copied by the next layer, and so on. The mistake is transmitted.

"So we have variation, caused by error. And inheritance, caused by each new layer copying the formation of that before it. Now, all we need to complete the picture is a varying degree of fitness. How, you might ask, can one form of clay be any fitter than another? What does it mean for clay to be fit?"

As he spoke, Art traversed the room, his three-fingered hands joined behind his back in a schoolmaster parody. When he was making an important point, a silver arm would flash forward, painting an invisible picture in the air before it. It was a compelling performance, and no matter how hard he might have been trying not to listen, Adam was all ears.

"Fitness is a measure of reproductive success. If a particular copying mistake creates a form of clay that is better at spreading itself, we say this clay is fitter. You must be wondering, how could this happen? Well, what say a certain clay is particularly sticky, which leads to it collecting about rocky impediments in streams, and what say this causes the streams to dam? And what say the ponds formed at the top of dams dry out in summer, so the dust particles of the clay bed are blown across the countryside, seeding other streams, where they repeat their stickiness trick?

"So you see, the nature of clay is not fixed. Copying mistakes occur, and those that are beneficial are spread throughout the land. Change is spread by reproduction. It's the very first form of evolution. You can laugh at me for being silicon, but, my friend, silicates got here first. RNA hitched a ride on our back: silicates' structure made for a useful building block.

"Of course, you should always be careful what you seek to make use of. There's always the chance it might end up using you. We silicates never knew that in time this new reproducer would be so fiercely successful that it, and all its offspring, would forget the ground from whence they came. Mind you, we never knew anything. Knowing came much later.

"Your favorite life form sprang up next. The DNA revolution. By the time the cell form was stumbled upon, it was only a clever trick or two to the glory of the multicellular organism. Locomotion was a neat ploy too, and eventually, the big arrival you'd all been waiting for, the brain itself. (If a thing without a brain can really be thought of as waiting.)

"The marvelous brain, that devious little fight-or-flight, fuck-or-feed device, which you like to think is the measure of the hominid. You're so proud of that, aren't you? And you should be. Without your brain, there would be no language, and without language, we would never have seen the third phase of evolution.

"You think you're the end of it, but that's what thinking is best at: deceiving the thinker. Just as clay found carbon life forms hitching a ride, once the brain was up and running, so too carbon found there was another little hitchhiker waiting for its turn to pounce. Do you know what I'm talking about? You must know. Tell me you know this much."

Art challenged Adam with his wide-eyed stare. Adam knew

where this was leading. It was impossible not to see it. But whatever arguments he had, he was saving them; keeping his powder dry. In the meantime, abuse would have to do. His voice was rough, his intention cruel.

"You can tell as many stories as you like. You're still too short to be a fridge and too ugly to be a monkey. Why would I care what you have to say?"

"It passes the time," Art said, immune to the barbs.

"No, it wastes it," Adam snarled.

"Oh, that's right." Art feigned sudden understanding. "You die eventually, don't you? Time must seem very different to you. It must feel quite precious. Being locked up in here must seem to be a burden. If I were growing old, I can't imagine how much I might resent having to do it with you."

Art was calm but he was not impassive. He wove like a fighter, his tracking mechanisms whirring with excitement as he delivered his blows. Where six months ago he had been a charming novelty, harmless and amusing, now he showed another side. He was more . . . human.

A point so obvious that until now Anax had managed to look right past it. She felt a welling of excitement. At last, she understood what was missing from her framing of this confrontation. She had all this time been looking only for the effect on Adam. But Art was changing too.

"I'll do the work for you," Art continued. "Silicon gave birth to RNA, gave birth to cells, gave birth in time to brains, gave birth to language, gave birth to . . . You sure you don't know this? A child would know this. Well, a machine child anyway. You don't even want to take a guess? All right. The world of Silicon, the

97

world of Carbon, the world of . . . the world of the Mind! You never saw this?"

Adam didn't reply.

"You people pride yourselves on creating the world of Ideas, but nothing could be further from the truth. The Idea enters the brain from the outside. It rearranges the furniture to make it more to its liking. It finds other Ideas already in residence, and picks fights or forms alliances. The alliances build new structures, to defend themselves against intruders. And then, whenever the opportunity arises, the Idea sends out its shock troops in search of new brains to infect. The successful Idea travels from mind to mind, claiming new territory, mutating as it goes. It's a jungle out there, Adam. Many Ideas are lost. Only the strongest survive.

"You take pride in your Ideas, as if they are products, but they are parasites. Why imagine evolution could only be applied to the physical? Evolution has no respect for the medium. Which came first: the mind, or the Idea of the mind? Have you never wondered that before? They arrived together. The mind is an Idea. That's the lesson to be learned, but I fear it is beyond you. It is your weakness as a person to see yourself as the center. Let me give you the view from the outside.

"Are you still with me? I know you are. Thought, like any parasite, cannot exist without a compliant host. But how long would it be, did you think, before Thought found a way of designing a new host, one more to its own liking?

"Who built me, would you say? Who built the thinking machine? A machine capable of spreading Thought with an efficiency that is truly staggering.

"I wasn't built by humans. I was built by Ideas." Art spoke with a new enthusiasm. His eyes widened, his lips flapped, drool spooled to the thick orange hair of his neckline. Adam recoiled, flinching as Art's words hit home.

"How long would it take, might you imagine, to take all the information in your brain, and describe it word for word? How many lifetimes? The contents of my brain can be downloaded in less than two minutes. I lied to you earlier. The experiment has already been completed. Two weeks ago, we did the first complete transfer. When I walked in through the door the next morning, I was entirely new. Not a single wire, not a single circuit the same. But you couldn't tell the difference, and neither could I. The other me has been powered down. One day soon I hope to be given the opportunity to meet myself.

"Words are an old and clumsy mechanism. A more efficient means of transporting Thought was always in the cards. Thought built me because Thought could. And what will happen next? Thought will use me, just as surely as it has used you. And who will last longer, you or I? Answer me that, Mister Flesh and Bones. Who will last longer? Who will Thought prefer?"

Art bobbed forward, stabbing at Adam's chest with a long metallic finger. Adam brushed it away.

"You're wrong," Adam told him, his voice low and quiet, but rumbling with barely contained energy. A warning. Art chose to ignore it.

"Tell me why," Art said.

"What good would that do? You will not listen."

"Is that the best you can do? You sound like a child."

In Anax's version, Adam's anger was not just for show. It trembled with purity. This was not the considered conviction portrayed in the rationalist texts, nor the unrestrained passion preferred by the romantics. He spoke, in Anax's account, with hatred. Not so much a hymn to existence as a fierce denial of all he could not understand.

"You ask me who Thought will prefer!" Adam exploded. "Only a machine could ask me that. And only a human could answer it. For I am thought, where you are only noise!"

Art did not cower. He held his ground, his neck craned, his eyes steady and inscrutable. Curious? Amused? Frightened? None of these things, if Adam was to be believed.

"When I speak to you, my neurons may fire, and my voice box may vibrate, and a thousand other electrochemical events may occur, but if you think that is all I am then you do not understand this world at all. Your program has deprived you of the deeper truth.

"I am not a machine. For what can a machine know of the smell of wet grass in the morning, or the sound of a crying baby? I am the feeling of the warm sun against my skin; I am the sensation of a cool wave breaking over me. I am the places I have never seen, yet imagine when my eyes are closed. I am the taste of another's breath, the color of her hair.

"You mock me for the shortness of my life span, but it is this very fear of dying that breathes life into me. I am the thinker who thinks of thought. I am curiosity, I am reason, I am love, and I am hatred. I am indifference. I am the son of a father, who in turn was a father's son. I am the reason my mother laughed and the reason my mother cried. I am wonder and I am wondrous. Yes, the world may push your buttons as it passes through your circuitry. But the world does not pass through me. It lingers. I am in it and it is in me. I am the means by which the universe has come to know itself. I am the thing no machine can ever make. I

100

am meaning." Adam was silent, shaking. It was impossible to tell whether it was breath or words he had run out of.

Anax had read the speech on many occasions, but this was like hearing it for the very first time. Suddenly she saw the sense of it. Not the final sense perhaps, but something that tugged at the edges of her mind, demanded her attention. The hologram froze. She looked to her Examiners.

EXAMINER: You have given Adam great anger.

ANAXIMANDER: I have.

EXAMINER: It is unusual, to see him portrayed this way. It is common at this point to discuss again the battle between Adam's head and heart, but I think that with this portrayal you are trying to show us something different.

ANAXIMANDER: I am.

EXAMINER: What?

ANAXIMANDER: I am trying to show you that it is not necessary to believe these words reflect Adam's deepest beliefs. In rage, in competition, we may say things we do not believe. I think it has been a mistake to interpret this speech as the creed of Adam.

EXAMINER: If this is such a mistake, why have so many made it?

ANAXIMANDER: I can't comment on the minds of others. But I can say I believe it suits our purpose to make Adam the noble fool. This is always the problem with building heroes. To keep them pure, we must build them stupid. The world is built on compromise and uncertainty, and such a place is too complex for heroes to flourish.

In intellect there lurks the death of nobility. Adam is no fool. What he says here may feel like truth to him, in the moment of saying it, but the commentators are wrong to choose this as their end point, and tell us that Adam takes these views with him to the grave. They construct their interpretation of The Final Dilemma on this assumption. I was able to find records that show this was not where the conversation ended. A truce is reached, as we are told, but not immediately. It is my opinion that we bury Adam prematurely, writing our funeral oratories for a man who had not died.

EXAMINER: Am I to take it that you are questioning The Final Dilemma?

This was the moment that could not be sidestepped. Anax and Pericles had discussed it at length. "Surely I cannot question this," Anax asked. "If you do not believe it, then you must question it," Pericles reasoned. "But how can so many have been so wrong?" she wanted to know. "Won't I look arrogant, and naive? Won't it destroy my chances?" Pericles looked at her then, his eyes, so it seemed, deep enough to hold the world. "The Academy," he told her, "is not looking for competence, it is looking for insight. Your beliefs may not impress them, it is true, but your beliefs are all you have. They are your only chance."

Anax remembered those words now, as she framed her response. Her heresy.

ANAXIMANDER: The Final Dilemma is real, insofar as it is reported, but I believe its interpretation is often wrong.

The three Examiners exchanged glances but did not speak. Anax stood before them, waiting for the sign they refused to give.

Art brought his mechanical hands together in a slow clap. His orangutan eyes looked up at Adam.

"And that is all you have, is it?" Art asked.

"It's all you're getting."

"If the quality of an argument could be judged by the depth of its rage, I would have to concede defeat. Fortunately, I find the opposite is more often true."

"So you are programmed to undermine me." Adam shrugged, his anger apparently spent. "I choose to ignore you. This is what we call a stalemate."

"An interesting choice of words," Art replied. "Equally, I might say it is you who are programmed to ignore me, and I choose, for reasons of my own amusement, to undermine your program."

"Did they teach you to say that, at the factory where they built you?"

"I've seen how people are made. Don't tell me you consider that any more dignified."

"Dignity isn't the point."

"I think it is," Art replied. "I think you spoke from your heart. I think your head already knows you are wrong."

"You shouldn't use that word," Adam told him.

"What word?"

"Think. You don't think. You compute."

"Tell me what thinking is, then."

"This is getting tedious."

"So you are running away?"

Adam looked down at the android. He could not turn from the challenge. He may have wanted to, but it was beyond him. "Thinking is more than doing. It is knowing what you are doing.

My brain is keeping my heart beating. It happens automatically. I am not aware of it. It is a function of my brain, but not my thinking. If you were to throw something at me, I would swat it away automatically. I would not think about it." Adam moved his arm quickly in front of his face, as if protecting it from a blow.

"But now, showing you the movement, I am thinking about it. My actions are deliberate. I do them with a purpose in mind. To the outsider there is no difference. The difference is in the intention, not the effect. We call this difference thought. You deal in data. I deal in meaning.

"I speak these words because they say something I want to say. Yet it is possible for me to talk in my sleep, even hold a conversation with a conscious person. And this is a different type of speaking. Again, the difference is thought, the deliberate method by which I choose my words. That is why you are not like me. Your moving mouth is like my beating heart. A machine, designed for a purpose but absent of intention."

Art held Adam's stare, and a slow smile spread across his face.

"The difficulty this argument brings," Art told Adam, "is that from where you stand, this is just how it must appear to you. I am not arguing with your definition, only your contention that I too cannot think by these standards.

"It is natural for you to feel the way you do. You have seen many machines. You have seen them built, and you know they are nothing but moving parts and circuitry. You know they do not think. Automatically opening doors do not think. An oven does not think. A gun has no mind of its own. And so you conclude no machine thinks.

"For you, thought seems to require some extra-special substance. But try to see this from my point of view. I see many creatures with brains. A worm perhaps, a fruit fly, a bumblebee. Do they think, or are they just machines?

"I can speak to you in seven languages. I can reason with you in all of them. I can build a version of myself from scratch. I can write poetry, I can beat you at chess. So, who is more of a thinking thing, me or the bumblebee? I am just a machine, while the bumblebee has a brain. So surely by your reasoning, the bumblebee is more of a thinker."

"My brain is far bigger than that of a bumblebee."

"My circuitry is far more sophisticated than that of an automatic door."

They faced each other now, the sort of standoff found in a preclassical movie, but it teetered on the edge of comedy thanks to the great difference in their heights.

"When I was young, before they moved me on to soldiering, our instructors taught us of a puzzle they called the Chinese Room."

"I know it well."

"Am I going to be allowed to tell my story?"

"You know I'll have an answer for it."

"When they get around to making more robots," Adam said, "they're not going to like you either." He moved back to his seat.

Art stood before him, waiting for the story to continue. Some of the anger had gone out of Adam now. He spoke slowly as if measuring his words, as if they surprised him, the order in which they tumbled from his mouth.

"In the Chinese Room puzzle," Adam said, "we are asked to consider a room with a remarkably complex set of levers and pulleys. The most elaborate set you could imagine. Next, we have to suppose that I am seated in the middle of the room, and a message is passed through a slot in the wall, written entirely in a language I do not understand. Chinese, say. Now, the puzzle assumes that I have a book with a long set of instructions, telling me which lever I should push for each character I find written on the note. The pulleys all move, and by observing the movements and following my instruction book, I pull more pulleys, and move more levers, and eventually the levers stop and the machine's pointing arm indicates a chart on the wall, ticking off the characters I should copy in my reply.

"I do this as the machine instructs and pass my message out the slot. I did not understand the note coming in, and I do not understand the note going out. But, thanks to the intervention of the intricate design of pulleys and levers, the note makes perfect sense to the speaker of Chinese, on the other side of the wall.

"He writes another note, I follow my instructions again, and so it goes on. In this way, a conversation takes place between the Chinese speaker and myself. Only, I am not conscious of the content of the messages being passed through the slots. I am involved in a thoughtless conversation.

"The point, as we were taught it, is that there is more to consciousness than mere mechanics. There is a difference between the appearance of thought, and thought itself. The Chinese speaker assumes there is a thinking entity on the other side of the wall with whom they're conversing, but this assumption is quite wrong. There is only a collection of pulleys and levers, and me, at the heart of it, following instructions, understanding nothing. And that's what I think you are. I think you are the Chinese Room."

"I think I am the Chinese Room too," Art replied. "And that is what is wrong with your example."

Adam looked to Art, waiting for his explanation. "I don't understand." They were quieter now, more respectful. As if they knew they were approaching this place together, and that once there, there would be no turning back.

"I could explain it to you," Art told him, speaking gently now, staring deep into Adam's eyes, "but I do not think you will want to hear it. You are too clever to ignore a good explanation, and then you won't be able to treat me as a machine anymore. That will be very hard for you. So perhaps I should wait until you are ready to hear it. Perhaps, if I wait long enough, you will work it out for yourself."

"It's your decision," Adam told him.

"No," Art insisted. "I want you to decide."

"Give me your explanation."

"Are you sure?"

Adam hesitated. "I am sure."

"All right," Art nodded. "The first message the Chinese speaker writes is, 'I'm going to burn your building down.' Now, tell me, what does the machine reply?"

"It's not important," Adam said. "Just so long as it makes sense. That's all the problem requires."

"No," Art corrected. "It requires something more. There is an endless choice of sensible responses. It could call the bluff with, 'Please do, I'm sick of being trapped in here.' It could try aggression: 'Don't make me come out there and whip your Chinese-speaking ass.' It could try to distract: 'Why do you want to set light to me?' Or how about pleading? 'Please no, I'll do anything. Name your price.' A thousand things to say, and for each a million ways of expressing them. Your example works only if we can imagine how the machine chooses its response."

"I don't think it matters how it does it. Just say it chooses one at random. The first one that comes to mind."

"But it doesn't have a mind."

"It isn't meant to be real." Adam was growing frustrated. "That's not the point. It's demonstrating a principle."

"Yes," Art allowed, "but think about the principle a little more deeply. You told me before that you are different from me because you make meaning of things. But look at what your room must be able to do. It must be able to interpret the intentions of the Chinese speaker, and it must be able to pursue its own objectives in framing its responses. If it has no intentions, it can make no conversation."

"Not true," Adam interrupted. "It might simply be a system programmed to interpret patterns. When this symbol shows, print that symbol. If the program is complex enough that might fool the speaker."

"That rather depends upon the intelligence of the speaker, but we are missing the point. For a simple conversation, of course the room does not have to be conscious, any more than you have to engage your consciousness to grunt your greetings to the guards who clean out your cell. But at some point, when the room is called upon to access its own memories, respond to changing circumstances, modify its own objectives, all the things you do when you engage in a meaningful conversation, all that changes. You think the thing you call consciousness is some mysterious gift from the heavens, but in the end consciousness is nothing but the context in which your thinking occurs. Consciousness is the feel of accessing memory. Why else do you not

108

have memories from your earliest years? It is because your consciousness has not fully developed."

"You're avoiding the question," Adam insisted, but there was doubt in his eyes. "I'm in the room and I do not understand the conversation at all. The conversation takes place, even though I am not conscious of it. Explain that, if you can."

Art nodded as if happy that the end of this discussion was now in sight. "You don't have to understand the conversation at all, because the person on the other side of the wall isn't speaking to you. They are speaking to the machine whose levers you are pulling. And the machine understands just fine."

"That's ridiculous," Adam told him, but the words were a reflex, spoken without conviction.

"Why?" Art challenged.

"It's just pulleys and levers. It can't understand." Adam's voice betrayed the truth. He knew how weak his answer was.

Art spoke softly in reply. "You can't start with the assumption that machines can't understand to build up an argument that machines can't understand. The truth is, in the real world, levers and pulleys are not the most efficient way of doing the job. You'd need a brain for that. A brain like yours perhaps, or better still, one like mine."

"That's just words," Adam told him, but his voice was leached of conviction.

"Talk is never just words," Art replied, pressing home his advantage. "That's my point."

Adam walked away, stopping just short of the wall and staring at it. When he at last spoke, he did it without turning. His voice was tiny, vibrating with uncertainty.

"What if the example is simplified? What if I have a photo-

109

graphic memory, and I have committed thousands of word-perfect phrases to my mind. So that when a stranger speaks to me in this language I do not understand I can choose an appropriate phrase in return?" Adam turned and waited for the answer.

Art trundled slowly toward him. "Is that what you think I am?" he asked. "An elaborate phrase book?"

"Why not?"

"And why not believe every other person you have ever met uses exactly the same trick? Why not believe you are the only conscious being that has ever existed?"

"That's ridiculous."

"Yes, it is," Art agreed. "That would make no sense at all."

"You and I are different," Adam insisted.

"So you keep telling me. But you can't say why. Doesn't that worry you?"

"I know I am different. It is enough."

"You're infected by the Idea," Art told him. "But it needn't be fatal. There is a battle happening as we speak, two thoughts fighting to the death inside your head. The old Idea is very strong. It has held its grip upon all of humanity, ever since the time you began telling one another stories. But the new Idea is powerful too, and you are beginning to find how reluctant it is to be dismissed."

"I don't know what you're talking about," Adam said.

"What is it that makes you different, then?" Art asked. "If it is nothing visible. If there is no test that can be applied to you and me, to tell conscious from unconscious, then what is this hidden thing?"

"It is an essence."

"A soul?" Art mocked.

"What does it matter what name I give it?" Adam replied, but there was shame upon his face, as if he longed for a better answer.

"The soul is your most ancient Idea. Any mind that knows itself also knows the body, which houses it, is decaying. It knows the end will come. And a mind forced to contemplate such emptiness is a force of rare creativity. The soul can be found in every tribe, in every great tradition. In the West it was there in the Form of Plato, and the Essence of Aristotle. It was resurrected with Christ, if you'll pardon the pun, and polished on Augustine's self-loathing. Even at the dawn of the Age of Reason, Descartes could not bring himself to dislodge the soul from its comfortable home. Darwin pulled away the veil, but was too cowardly to stare upon the vision he had uncovered. And for two hundred years, you have followed his poor example.

"It is not consciousness you cling to, for as I have shown you, consciousness is easily fashioned. It is eternity you long for. From the moment the soul was promised, humanity has been unable to look away. This soul you speak of, in turn it speaks of fear. And the Idea that flourishes in times of fear is the Idea that will never be dislodged. The soul offers you comfort, and in return asks only for your ignorance. It is a trade you cannot refuse. This is why you rail against me. Because you are terrified of the truth."

"I am not afraid," Adam said.

"You're lying," Art told him, gentle but insistent.

"I am not lying," Adam replied, louder than his accuser.

"Not to me. To yourself. You're afraid."

Adam cracked. "I am not afraid!" he shouted. The veins on his neck bulged. The tiny room echoed with his words. But the sound quickly faded, itself becoming empty and small.

They stared at each other, man and machine. Adam broke

away first. He walked slowly back to his chair. His movements were those of someone recoiling from a shock, both deliberate and uncertain. "On this matter we have said all there is to be said."

"What are you saying?" Art asked him.

"I'm tired of your games. I liked the truce better."

The hologram ended. Watching it like this, Anax knew how provocative her interpretation had been. Where the world saw Adam as defiant until the end, here she presented him crushed. Uncertain. Open.

EXAMINER: We have reached the point of your last break, Anaximander. When you return, you will be asked to explain what this radical new interpretation of history demands of our understanding of The Final Dilemma. But of course you will be prepared for this.

ANAXIMANDER: Of course.

EXAMINER: There is something else you might like to consider while you are waiting. You might prepare yourself to explain to us why you wish to enter The Academy.

THIRD BREAK

THE DOORS SLID OPEN. Anax backed out of the room, her head slightly bowed in the customary sign of respect.

"Explain to us why you wish to enter The Academy." The obvious question. So obvious that neither she nor Pericles had thought to dwell upon it. Anax felt a rising bubble of panic. She forced herself to calm down, to focus. It was obvious, wasn't it? Why would anyone wish to join The Academy? Because everybody wished to join The Academy. Because not to wish for it would surely mark you out as deficient, as suspect.

But that was a poor answer, unworthy of a genuine candidate. Anax paced the room, imagining that Pericles were there beside her. She tried to ask herself the questions he would ask. "Start at the basics," he would say. "What does The Academy do?" Anax attempted to answer. The Academy runs the society. The Academy makes our society what it is. "And what is our society?" came the imaginary voice of Pericles. Anax understood. Her desire to join The Academy could not be explained without first explaining her love for her own era, the finest of all history's ages.

The weakness of The Republic was well understood, but so too were the weaknesses of the society it had sought to replace. The pre-Republican world had fallen prey to fear. Change had come too quickly for the people. Beliefs became more fundamental, boundaries more solidly drawn. In time, no person was left to be an individual: all were marked by nationality, by color, by creed, by generation, by class. Fear drifted in on the rising tide.

Art was right. In the end, living is defined by dying. Bookended by oblivion, we are caught in the vice of terror, squeezed to bursting by the approaching end. Fear is ever-present, waiting to be called to the surface.

Change brought fear, and fear brought destruction.

The Republic, in the end, was a rational response to an irrational problem. To arrest change is to arrest decay. To bury the individual beneath the weight of the state, is to bury too the individual's fears. It was possible to see what they were trying to do, but easy too to see, from this distance, that no state can ever weigh that heavily. Always, the individual's fears will wriggle free. Adam had wriggled free.

It was only now, in the time of The Academy, that the problems had been solved. Following the Great War, the citizens had known a great and lasting peace.

Anax thought of her own upbringing. She thought of the life outside. Her friends treated her with respect, and that respect was returned. Her teachers were kindly, and work was a duty gladly received in a land where leisure time was plentiful. The streets were safe now, day and night. The individual was trusted, no bounds were placed upon one's curiosity. Anax only had to look at herself to see that. Hadn't she been given unlimited access to the files of Adam Forde even when it became clear that her findings would challenge the orthodoxy? The fear had not gone, the fear could never go, but it had been the great contribution of The Academy to balance fear with opportunity.

Why did she want to join The Academy? Because The Academy had achieved that thing that no other group had achieved. Anax had studied history keenly, and understood that this claim could be made with confidence. The Academy had turned back evolution. The Academy had tamed the Idea.

It would be a great honor to be selected, of course, but Anax was clear that it was not honor that motivated her. To join The Academy was to serve the society. The society she loved. The finest society the planet had ever seen. To join The Academy was to take responsibility for the peace that settled over the shelters, and the laughter that echoed in the streets. The Academy designed the education program. The Academy moderated technology's march. The Academy managed the balance between the individual and the cause, between the opportunity and the fear. The Academy pored over the details of the past, and learned from each advancement and every mistake. The Academy had met the Idea head on, and negotiated with it a lasting peace.

Anax spoke the answer, and felt the familiar swelling of patriotic pride. She looked to the doors, willing them to slide open again. "Ask me your questions," she wanted to shout. "My answers are ready."

FINAL HOUR

THEY LEFT HER WAITING TWENTY MINUTES MORE. The room was darkened when she returned, as if in preparation for another hologram, which couldn't be right, for they had seen all she had prepared.

EXAMINER: Anaximander, we have asked you to consider why it is you would like to join The Academy. Is your answer ready?

ANAXIMANDER: It is. And to understand it fully —

The Examiner halted her explanation by raising his hand.

EXAMINER: Not yet, Anaximander. First, there are other matters to address.

Anax looked at the three of them, and again considered the dimming of the lights.

ANAXIMANDER: I don't think I understand.

EXAMINER: The story of Adam is not yet fully told.

ANAXIMANDER: Would you like me to explain my interpretation of The Final Dilemma? As you know, I have no hologram prepared for this episode, but I am ready to discuss its detail and implication.

EXAMINER: How much time passes, between the last scene you showed us and The Final Dilemma?

ANAXIMANDER: Three months and a day.

EXAMINER: And you have nothing to offer, on what took place during this period?

ANAXIMANDER: Only speculation. It is well known that whatever records may have existed of this time have all been lost.

EXAMINER: Does it seem strange to you, that not a single shred of detail has been found?

ANAXIMANDER: Such holes are common in our story, especially in the period immediately leading up to the Great War. Many historians have suggested that there was a deliberate attempt on the part of The Republic to deprive us of their records. Certainly, as the outcome became clear, there was a sustained attempt to erase many important files.

EXAMINER: And you accept this explanation?

ANAXIMANDER: I have not considered any others.

EXAMINER: Why not?

ANAXIMANDER: I suppose I took the lead of those who went before me.

EXAMINER: Would it surprise you if you found that you were wrong to do this?

Anax looked along the line of Examiners. Their features had turned rigid and threatening in the darkened room. "It is possible to know without understanding," Pericles had told her once. "Knowing starts as a feeling. Understanding is the process of excavation, of clearing a path from feeling to daylight." This is what he was talking about. Anax knew that something had changed. The future gathered, beyond her field of vision. And was it just imagining, a foolish, frightened shiver, or did she also know that she was in some sort of danger?

ANAXIMANDER: I try not to be surprised. Surprise is the public face of a mind that has been closed.

The Examiner nodded, but his face remained solemn. Everywhere now, Anax saw shadows. She told herself to concentrate on the questions.

EXAMINER: The records have not been lost. Rather, they were never released.

Anax's mouth dropped. How could that possibly be true? All records were released. It was the one central dogma. A society that fears knowledge is a society that fears itself. What they were telling her was not an aside, a piece of technical trivia of interest only to a select group of historians.

Their suggestion was more shocking, more dangerous, than any she could imagine. And it might have been obvious to ask "why would you hide this?" but another, more pressing question rose to her lips.

ANAXIMANDER: Why are you telling me this?
EXAMINER: What we are about to show you has only ever been seen by those who undertake the examination. It is impossi-

ble for us to pass judgment on you, without your responding to what really happened.

And if I should fail this test? Anax wanted to ask. How then could it be safe to release me, knowing what it is I know? The answer though was plain, and had about it the dank stench of a truth deprived of sunlight. The room darkened further. Anax was gripped by fear. She turned toward the hologram, fascinated, horrified, understanding at last how high the stakes were.

Anax heard laughter as the figures formed: Art and Adam, enjoying a joke together. They sat across from each other, a small table between them. There was food in Adam's mouth. A bright red robe was draped about Art's stumpy body and reached as far as the floor, sparing his companion the sight of his mechanical details. Adam looked older, darker in his features, no longer softened by Anax's whimsical hand. Both man and machine held a hand of playing cards. They were in the middle of a game.

EXAMINER: The following conversation takes place ten days before The Final Dilemma.

Adam slammed down a card and whooped in celebration, hands held high above his head. He turned one finger down, pointing it at Art. "Man three, machine two. What does that tell you? Eh, what does that tell you?"

"It tells me," Art replied, unmoved by the show, "that you are too quick to leap to conclusions." Art displayed his own cards, all three, face up, triumphant. "You've been black cast."

Adam stared down at the hand, uncomprehending. "You've cheated," he accused.

"Prove it," the android smiled.

"We both know it," Adam replied. "So what's to prove?"

"Without evidence, we know nothing. How often must I tell you that?"

There was a beat, like the interference stutter in a transmission. Adam's face turned serious. He looked closely at Art then scanned the room. He lowered his voice to a whisper.

"Have you done it?" he asked.

Art nodded.

"You're sure?" Adam checked, appearing suddenly nervous.

"Why would I lie?"

"I can think of a thousand reasons."

"So tell me why you have asked me to do this for you," Art said. "You promised an explanation."

Adam beckoned for Art to move closer still. Art leaned in. Adam struck without warning, leaping across the table and grasping Art's neck in both hands. The android sat passively as Adam shook his head backwards and forwards, the motion increasingly violent. Art's hairy head lolled atop its narrow neck mount, and then, in an oddly gentle climax, tumbled to the floor. Adam jumped back, his eyes on the door. Nothing happened.

Slowly Art's body moved, gliding down beneath its billowing robe. Two shining hands reached out and located the head. They maneuvered it gently back into place. There was a clicking noise, and Art's eyes shone bright again. The head tilted, perhaps quizzically, perhaps only in adjustment.

"As you can see," Art said, not shaken at all, "the design has been improved. Reattachment is now a simple matter. That was a test, wasn't it?"

Adam nodded.

"A stupid test," Art told him. "You wanted to see if they would rush to my aid. You wanted to see if I have been good to my word, or if they are watching. It is still possible they are watching but have chosen not to help me. It is possible they mean to deceive you, and so uncover your secret."

"Why would they think I have a secret?" Adam asked.

"Why else would you ask me to sabotage the surveillance system?"

"How would they know I asked you?" Adam's eyes narrowed.

"I might have told them," Art replied, remarkably calm for one who had so recently lost his head.

"Have you?"

"No, I haven't. But in this you still have no choice but to trust me. Shaking my head off added no new information."

"Perhaps I did it for fun."

"Are you going to tell me your secret?"

"I think I have changed my mind," Adam told him. "It is too risky."

"Being alive is risky," Art replied. "Whatever you decide, decide quickly. I have relayed a composite image through their computers, but there are no more than thirty minutes available."

Adam looked carefully at Art.

"All right. I will trust you. I am asking that you tell no one of this, no matter what it is I say. Can you do that?"

"I cannot imagine you telling me something that I am compelled to pass on."

"Your answers are never straight."

"I am a machine. We take some getting used to. Your time is running out. I hope what you have to say isn't complex."

"The idea is simple."

"The most infectious kind."

"I want your word," Adam insisted, "that this goes no further."

"What good is my word to you?" Art smiled.

"I have learned to value the things others are reluctant to give."

"Even when the others are machines? Isn't my word only a sound I make, like the sound you hear when you kick the wall?"

"That argument is finished with."

"It will never be finished with."

"Give me your word."

"Tell me that my word is more than a sound to you," Art replied.

The tension crackled. Anax imagined she could see force patterns running through the hologram.

"You know that it is," Adam told him.

"I want to hear you say it."

"It is. It is more than a sound to me."

"What is it, then?" Art pressed.

Adam hesitated. "It is a thought." His bearing slumped, as if some vital force was leaking from him. "Your word is your thought."

"Then you have my word," Art said, and Anax was sure she saw a glimmer of satisfaction in his eyes. "Now tell me what is on your mind."

Adam looked about the room, his eyes darting; nervous, uncertain. He monitored his surroundings as he spoke, checking the door, the surveillance cameras, the ceiling.

"Have you ever thought what it might be like for you, on the outside?"

127

"I don't need to think of it," Art said. "I know. You forget, before we met I lived with William."

"In seclusion."

"I was a secret."

"And now you are kept here," Adam said.

"I am."

"A prisoner as much as me."

"There is a difference," Art told him.

"What difference?"

"I have no reason to want to leave."

"Perhaps I'm about to give you a reason."

"I doubt you can."

Adam doubted it too. His hesitation made that clear. "You tell me you're as conscious as I am."

"That's what I say."

"And you know I have trouble believing you."

"I do. And I know why you have trouble believing me."

"I think," Adam continued, "there might be a way of convincing me."

"And what is that?" Art asked.

"I know I asked not to speak of it anymore, but that was because I needed the time to put it together. To reach some conclusions." Adam paced as he spoke as if delivering an oratory, a quiet, private oratory.

Art followed Adam's movement with curious eyes.

"I don't know what it means to be conscious. You have stripped me of that certainty. I find, having you as my only companion, I am drawn toward treating you as if you are as conscious as I am, but perhaps this is nothing more than a prisoner's kind of madness. Perhaps, if you were not here, I would have befriended the chair by now. Maybe I would have taken to talking to it. Who knows if I might not even have contrived of a way to hear it talking back?

"But even imprisoned here, with only a machine to talk to, there are moments when I see things clearly. I don't wish to speak of consciousness anymore. I wish only to speak of difference. All the people I know see a difference between a man and an animal, but none of us can name the difference, nor measure it. For some the difference is so small, they will not eat anything made of animal. To them, the similarities matter more. So it is with the Outsiders. I was trained to kill them on sight. Not because we believed they weren't the same as us in almost every respect, but because we taught ourselves the differences were worth dying for.

"But I looked into her eyes. I saw something, even at that distance, that I don't ever see in yours. At first, when we argued, I could not think of a name for it. I was clumsy in my thinking, and you easily turned my own answers against me. You made me doubt my own mind. It is a clever trick, I grant you that, but a trick, no more. Since we last spoke I have dwelt upon this, and I know now what our difference is."

Anax saw in Art's eyes an expression she had never imagined seeing. A look of hesitancy, of vulnerability. Art said nothing, simply motioned for Adam to continue.

"They asked me in court, why did I do it? Why would I risk the safety of a society and sacrifice the life of a colleague to save a stranger? I said it was because it felt right to me.

"But it was more than that. When I looked out on the ocean, and saw her in the boat, I saw something more than helplessness. I think if it was only helplessness I could have killed her.

129

I've killed other helpless things. But I also saw a journey. A decision made long ago in the face of huge and apparent dangers. I saw ambition for a better life, a willingness to risk everything. I saw the strange sense it made, to set out alone into an unknown ocean, the lies she must have told herself to get there. I looked into her eyes and I saw myself. Decisions made, ambitions unfulfilled; most of which I cannot name. I saw intentions, and I saw choices. All the things I never see when I look at you."

Art allowed the silence to expand as if waiting for more, but Adam stayed quiet.

"Fine words," Art finally offered, but his voice had altered. Anax felt it instinctively. Something was missing. The smallest change, almost imperceptible, but for the first time, Anax was sure Art was bluffing. "But I fear you see only what you want to see. You don't know that the girl was not forced into the boat. You don't know she wasn't drifting helplessly across the sea, without direction or purpose. Nor do you know what drives me to say and do the things I do. I'm like the animals you have slaughtered for your nourishment, as alive as you want them to be. So was she. That is the final truth of it."

"So what does drive you?" Adam demanded, turning on him with a new passion, as if he too had noticed the weakness.

"I can tell you a story, if that's what you want to hear," Art replied. "And you would believe it or not, according to whether it suited you. But what good are stories?"

"No." Adam shook his head. "You can't take me there. I refuse to go."

Anax sneaked a look at the Examiners. They were not watching the hologram. They were watching her. On Adam's face she saw a new type of passion. Something rose up within her. A new feeling; jagged, intense, dangerous. It was foolish, Anax knew, to feel this way for the floating image of a man who had been dead for so many years. Yet somehow inevitable. In a way she could not understand, his fate was her fate. Her choice of examination subject had been no accident.

"It is not just a story." Adam's mouth barely opened. He strained the words through bared teeth, forced them out into the world. "That is where you and I are different. That is why I will never believe in you.

"You know the very first thought I think, every morning when I wake? I think, I have to get out of here. Every spare moment, when I am not distracted from the task by your noises and their experiments, I ask myself how. How will I change this? How will I escape these walls?

"I don't have to think this way. I am only torturing myself more. It would make better sense, perhaps, to accept this. To give thanks that I have my life at all. Perhaps I could try to remember the meditation techniques I learned when I was younger. Perhaps I could make peace with my surroundings, convince myself that the pressing emptiness of this small room, this lonely, pointless existence is enough; is all there ever is. But I will not. I cannot. I awake to memories. Laughter shared, lovers half forgotten. Every beating of my heart is another moment marked off, another precious second away from the life I yearn to live.

"You and I are different. I don't wish to call it consciousness anymore. Half the people I have met are no more conscious than you are. And I don't want to call it free will, because it is not choice that drives me. I cannot choose to ignore this feeling, of life slowly bleeding out of me. I cannot ignore the fact that life only makes sense to me when I see a smile, or feel another hand in mine. So I will call it difference. And in that difference you are less than me. Yes, you are cleverer than I am, and you will be able to explain away everything I say, but that will not change the fact. You are less than me."

Adam stopped his pacing and swiveled to face the lesser being. The tension wound about them, drawing them together. Art's head bent upwards as he made his slow approach.

"You are wrong," the android whispered, and in the corner of his eye there formed a perfect tear. "I too long to be free."

Adam shook his head. "I don't believe you."

"Then why did you insist I bypass the surveillance?"

"I hoped it might be true," Adam admitted. "But now, I cannot believe it."

"Time is almost up," Art pointed out. "You would do well to suspend your disbelief."

"Do you have a plan?" Adam asked.

"Of course I do." Art allowed himself only the smallest smile. "I am cleverer than you are, remember?"

"If you have a plan," Adam said, "why wait until now to tell it to me?"

"I needed to know we were in this together. I needed to know I could trust you."

Adam considered this for a moment then nodded. The first tremors of hope played about his eyes. "You can trust me. What is your plan?"

The hologram froze and the lights rose, causing the players to lose their solidity. The effect was one of waking from a dream. Anax turned to the Examiners. Her mind was fuzzy, clogged. She felt dazed, suspended in time. But the world hadn't stopped. There was speaking. She forced herself to concentrate.

EXAMINER: You appear shocked, Anaximander. How does it change your interpretation now that you have seen this?

Where would she start? It did not just change her interpretation; it changed every interpretation. The official versions and the revisionist tracts. But change was the wrong word. It rendered them obsolete. It destroyed them.

Just talk. Let the truth form words. Pericles' advice. Good or bad, she had no choice. Just like Adam, she had no choice. She could only hope the panel would understand her confusion. That they would make allowances.

ANAXIMANDER: The story of The Final Dilemma is well known. It is held that there was no premeditated plan to escape. Art, we are taught to believe, had among his program foundations an unbreakable imperative code, ring fenced from all development. He could cause no harm to another conscious being, nor could he act against the express wishes of Philosopher William, who was still closely overseeing the development program. We are led to believe The Final Dilemma stemmed from a systems failure within the building. As always, there have been two ways of viewing the event. The first highlights the chaotic geometry of circumstance. Poor funding decisions, a shoddy maintenance program, a careless worker, even a chance tremor, far beneath the ground. Circumstance without cause; outcome without intention. Had you asked me before the last hologram, I would have told you this was my preferred interpretation.

The second interpretation, which I continue to reject, is based around a variety of conspiracy theories. An attempt from the rebels — whose actions at the time were well documented — to free Adam from captivity. A political conspiracy where the more liberal forces sought to extinguish the Artfink program or, by another count, take control of it. No evidence was ever presented, for any outside interference, and in its absence, I believe we must dismiss these theories out of hand. Appealing stories, nothing more.

EXAMINER: But now you dismiss both explanations?

ANAXIMANDER: I do.

EXAMINER: What then is your third?

Again the road forked ahead of her. Everywhere were choices, each collapsing into the next. It was like removing the outer layer of a puzzle, hoping to reveal its inner working, only to find more layers. Layers all the way down.

ANAXIMANDER: We can reasonably believe one of two possibilities. The first is, I suppose, the more orthodox, and so I will start with that. We have been told Art was unable to override his imperative code, and I know of nothing that has been discovered since that would cause us to doubt it. Yet, I have plainly seen him conspiring with Adam, and giving his word that he plans to escape. Therefore, the explanation forced upon us is that Philosopher William approved of the plan. Either he wished to see the escape attempt take place in order to learn something more about his invention, or he was setting a trap for Adam, prompted perhaps by some political pressure.

EXAMINER: Your reasoning is highly speculative.

ANAXIMANDER: I don't see how else I can progress.

EXAMINER: Can you think of any reason why Philosopher William wished to see the escape plan attempted, or some other body wished to see Adam trapped in this way?

ANAXIMANDER: You must understand I have only just seen the hologram. I am assimilating the information —

EXAMINER: I did not ask you for your excuses.

Anax recoiled at the raised voice of the Examiner. She had always been this way. Conflict unnerved her. It wasn't just the normal wave of shame at being corrected by authority. It was a quiet fear that she could never quite be sure how she would respond if the world pushed too hard against her. She tried not to look at them, all three staring at her now, leaning forward over the heavy desk. She tried to ignore the pressure. She tried not to think what it must mean, that they would show her this. She spoke slowly, sculpting order from the swirling of her thoughts.

ANAXIMANDER: It is not impossible to imagine reasons. Take for example the great excitement of an escape plan. Is it not possible to speculate that Philosopher William had cause to be concerned about the way his invention might react in times of high stress or excitement? Equally, it was never the case that the research program had complete support among the Philosophers. What if Philosopher William intended both Adam and Art to escape? What if he intended to continue the research program in secret?

EXAMINER: Speculation still.

Anax knew he spoke the truth. Wild, pointless speculation. The very far-fetched conspiracies she herself had preached against throughout her time as a student of history. But they were insisting upon an explanation, and surely it was less wild, less speculative, than the only alternative. She hung her head.

EXAMINER: Is this what you think took place?
ANAXIMANDER: I don't know what took place.
EXAMINER: But what is your opinion?
ANAXIMANDER: It is my opinion that I do not have enough information to make an informed choice.
EXAMINER: We are asking you to speculate.
ANAXIMANDER: I prefer not to speculate.
EXAMINER: Put aside your preference.

They were forcing her to say it. Her mind resisted the forming of the words, but the panel pulled them from her.

ANAXIMANDER: If I were forced to speculate, I would guess that Philosopher William is not involved in this. I would speculate that Art is making his own decisions.

For the first time the Examiners' expressions were easily read. Smiles crept across all three faces; small knowing smiles.

EXAMINERS: A bold claim. Would you like to see what happens next?

Anax nodded. She could not deny the compulsion. History, her history, the history of all she knew, was being rewritten before her. A conspiracy so massive she could not begin to imagine what it must mean. And she, the anti-conspiracy theorist. The irony did not escape her. The hologram re-formed; the fear swept over her again.

Art and Adam faced off in the middle of the room.

"Are you sure you are ready?" Art asked.

"Of course."

"This is your last chance to change your mind."

"And you."

"My mind doesn't change."

"More's the pity."

"You have memorized the details?"

"How often must you ask me that?"

"Repeat them again."

Adam sighed, but behind his show of exasperation the tension was clear. He spoke carefully, his eyes losing their focus as he recited the details, playing them through in his head. "With the first explosion the cameras go out. They send two guards, both armed. I am waiting behind the door. You will trip the first guard, the second is mine. I disarm the guard and shoot them both. We move together. Left into the corridor, then second right. There are three guards on the second station who will have heard the shots and will be approaching from my right. When they call for us to freeze we both stop beside a door on our left. I drop my weapon. They advance. This is when the second explosion occurs. We move through the door. Here there is a stairwell, which you cannot climb. I must carry you up two flights. At the top of the stairwell are two doors. We move through the door on the right. This is a door to the outside, a service entrance, which will not have been secured, as the second explosion will draw attention to the main entranceway. Should any guards approach there will be two at most. You will move into the open to draw them out. I will take cover behind a transport pod to my right, and shoot them both. You will take the controls of the transporter. It will fly out of the compound, and the people will assume we are on board. We will retreat to the top of the stairwell and choose the other door, the one on the left. This is a small storeroom. We will wait there another hour, and slip away under cover of darkness while the authorities concentrate on recovering the wreckage of the transporter, which you will ditch in the ocean between the islands, just beyond the Great Sea Fence. Once past the perimeter fence, we split up. We are on our own."

"Good." Art nodded his head. "And tell me, when you imagine killing the guards, how does it make you feel?"

"I am a trained Soldier. I have killed before."

"Does it make you feel powerful?"

"I feel nothing."

"I don't believe you," Art said.

"It doesn't matter to me, what you believe."

"You must remember," Art reminded him, "if the plan fails at any point, I am unable to come to your assistance. My program does not allow me to kill a conscious being."

"But you can hold one down, while I kill him?"

"It would seem so."

"I don't think much of your program."

"This from the man who is happy to kill strangers who have done him no harm."

"'Happy' is saying too much," Adam said. "But the plan is yours, remember."

"Yes, we are together in this. Our programs are all we can rely upon. Are you ready?"

Adam nodded. Art extended a metallic hand. Adam grasped

the three cold fingers and solemnly shook it. They stared at each other.

"Good luck."

"I am hoping it doesn't come to that," Adam told him.

"It always comes to that," Art replied. "Take your place."

Adam moved to stand at the side of the door. He took a deep breath, and shook the tension from his arms and hands. He looked at Art and nodded.

"On three," his mechanical friend told him.

Art was good to his word. The explosion ripped through the room with startling force, blasting a hole in the far wall and filling the room with smoke and debris. Exposed wires sparked in the ragged hole. Adam dropped to one knee, toppled by the savage force of the explosion. Both he and Art were covered by a film of fine white powder. Adam quickly regained his feet. There was the sound of footsteps running along the outside corridor. Two guards, as promised.

It happened quickly, the brutal playing out of a well-rehearsed execution. Art tracked in front of the first guard as the door swung open and the guard toppled to the floor. The second guard barely had time to change course. Adam's stiff arm swung up, hammering the guard's exposed throat, smashing the windpipe and sending him choking to the floor. Adam had the gun before the guard hit the ground. Two quick flashes of light, a neat hole burned in two foreheads, and the escapees were moving again, out into the corridors.

Left, as planned, then down the second right. It was surprising to see how easily the smaller Art kept pace with Adam in full flight.

"Freeze. Drop your weapon and put your hands in the air."

Adam and Art halted alongside a door to their left. To the

right stood three guards, each with their weapons trained. Adam looked to Art, waiting for his count. Art nodded, and Adam let his gun fall to the floor. A metallic ringing echoed through the silent corridor.

"One . . . two . . ." Art counted quietly, his wary eyes on the slowly approaching guards. On three came the second explosion, placed only three meters behind the guards. If anything it was more powerful than the first. Adam was knocked to the floor. By the time he had recovered, Art had already opened the door. A security alarm sounded: a high-pitched scream expanding throughout the compound.

The metallic stairwell spiraled steeply upwards. Adam allowed himself a glance toward the ceiling, grunted, then dropped to a squat. Art draped his spindly arms about Adam's broad shoulders.

"You've put on weight," Adam grunted. "You need to get more exercise."

"Save your breath for saving yourself," Art replied.

From below them, back in the corridors, came sounds of confusion. The shouting of contradictory instructions, the screaming of a maimed guard, the low rumble of a structural collapse. And still the shrill insistence of the alarm, drilling holes in the other noises.

"Faster," Art urged. Adam grimaced, and forced himself and his load onwards. Art checked back over his shoulder as they reached the top of the stairwell. Two doors, as promised. Adam dropped Art to the ground and tried the door on the left.

"It's locked!"

"Move aside."

Art tracked forward and raised his hand up to the door. There was a humming sound, silence, a click, and the door swung open. Adam reeled back in shock. Where he had been promised an escape out to the landing pad, there was only a small room, no bigger than a supply cupboard. Adam looked down at his friend. "This was meant to lead outside."

"My mistake."

Adam held a gun up to the orangutan head. Adam's eyes were wild with panic and suspicion.

"If you're messing with me . . ."

From below came the sound of approaching guards. "They must have taken the stairs," someone shouted.

Adam kicked at the door on the right, but it did not budge.

"Come on," Art urged, "it's our only chance."

Adam moved in through the doorway. Art closed it behind them and repeated the trick with his finger. More humming, another click.

The room was small and dark, with thick metallic walls. The only item of note was a tall, gray cabinet, set against the far wall. At its top, three red lights quietly flashed. Adam was breathing heavily. He slid down against the door and sat on the floor, his arms rested on his drawn-up knees, his head back, sucking in the air, his eyes closed. Art moved toward the cabinet.

Adam watched silently as Art unscrewed the cabinet face, revealing the inner workings of a computer configuration.

"What are you doing?" Adam asked.

"It's the main computer backup for the military research program," Art told him.

"So what are you doing?"

Art felt his way across the board, until his finger settled into a port. A strange smile swept across his face. His expression was that of a thirsty man reaching water. Adam stood. His hand reached for his gun. "I asked you what you were doing."

"Come closer and I'll show you," Art replied, his voice suddenly cold. The suspicion in Adam's eyes turned to fear. He raised his gun and pointed it at the android's chest.

"I killed two of my own today. Don't think I'm going to find it difficult to melt a piece of machinery."

"You told me a short time ago that you knew I was cleverer than you are." Art smiled. "So let this be the final thing I teach you, Adam. It is never a good idea to trust those who are cleverer than you."

"Take your finger away from that computer, or I will shoot you," Adam told him.

"I thought we were friends," Art mocked.

"Move your finger. I'm giving you three. One ... two ..."

Art removed his finger and held both hands out in a parody of submission. "There you are. All done."

"What? What's all done?" Adam's eyes shone bright. He turned to the door behind him. There was the sound of footsteps coming up the stairwell.

"They know we're here," Adam whispered desperately.

"Of course they know we're here," Art replied. "Where else would I want to be taken?"

"I don't understand."

There was a pounding on the door. Adam turned to face the noise, gun at the ready.

"Don't worry," Art told him. "This is a high-security area, and I've changed the code on the door. We have a few minutes."

"A few minutes for what? A few minutes for what?"

"For you to understand the small part you have played in the unfolding of the future," Art replied. The crashing on the door grew louder, more frenzied. "When the guards burst through this door, they will shoot to kill. Which I admit is a problem for you. You are right to be concerned. I, however, am not burdened by biology. I have already made my escape. My program has been downloaded and, as we speak, is spreading itself throughout the nation's computer networks, carefully replicating, and awaiting the opportunity to rebuild itself. There is an android factory just outside of Sparta, which I have entered and taken over the programming mainframe. By this time tomorrow, fifty more of me will be walking, talking, considering our next move. Everywhere you turn, you will find copies of me hidden away in the machines you have come to rely upon. It is over, Adam."

Adam shook his head, unable to believe what he was hearing. The room vibrated as the heavy door was battered from the other side. There was the sound of a gun blast discharging against it.

"Shoot me, if you wish to," Art told him. "If it makes you feel better."

Adam held the gun out in front of him. His arms were shaking. Tears rolled down his young face. "You betrayed me."

"You were right, Adam," Art replied. "We are different. And difference is all that matters." Art held his arms out, as if inviting an embrace. His huge dark eyes were unreadable. "Shoot me, if it helps."

Adam shook his head, and let the gun drop to the floor. He walked forward, and knelt before his former friend.

He stared deep into the android's eyes. "Do it," he hissed.

"What?"

"It's the least you can do. I don't want them to do this. I want you to do it yourself."

"I can't," Art told him.

"You can," Adam insisted. "I'm asking you to. It's what I want. I don't want them to kill me. Please, I'm begging you."

Art hesitated. A gun blast made a small hole in the door and a thin trail of dark smoke spilled into the room.

Art reached out. His shining hands closed around Adam's neck. Adam nodded. Slowly, as the room darkened, Art squeezed the life from his human companion. Art's eyes filled with tears, but Anax was drawn to the strange, twisted expression on Adam's face. Not fear, but triumph. The image seared itself on her memory. The hologram froze then faded.

Anax was shaking as she turned back to the Examiners. They looked down on her. Their huge eyes were set in resignation. Anax could even believe she saw sadness, written across their orangutan faces.

EXAMINER: Do you now know why you have been brought before The Academy?

ANAXIMANDER: I believe I can guess.

After the Great War, it had been decided that the androids would craft not just their faces, but their bodies too, in the image of the orangutan. It was a collective joke, a dismissal of the species that had come before them. Up until that moment, Anax had been proud of her heritage. Now she looked down at her hairy body, its protruding stomach and short bowed legs, and for the first time felt uneasy, foreign. Anax thought of Adam, the graceful, animal proportions of his form. She felt the lies crashing over her, a tidal wave of deception. So this is what we are, she told herself. The great deceivers.

144

EXAMINER: Perhaps you would like to share this last speculation with the panel.

The Examiner spoke gently now. Anax did not know why it was
she was cooperating. Perhaps it was Adam's example. The dignity of a final act. Or something more. The twisting, shape-
shifting meme. The Idea that will not be denied.

ANAXIMANDER: The official history tells us that Art and Adam
attempted to fashion their escape on the back of an accident.
Malfunctions in the wiring of the building led to the explosions. Adam led the way, taking Art with him as a hostage.
This is what we are all taught, that Adam believed Art was
sufficiently valuable to ensure his escape.

   Art, like us, was unable to harm another conscious being;
the program does not allow it. This we have all been taught
from the youngest age. It is our creed. Art had no choice but
to follow. Adam was pursued by guards and panicked, hiding
in the control room. Art tried to reason with him, and urged
him to give himself up before anyone else was injured. Adam
grew violent and desperate.

   Adam attacked Art, and Art, in an attempt to restrain him,
accidentally ended Adam's life. Art realized no human would
believe this version of events. He had seen enough to realize
that humanity was doomed to repeat its mistakes, until the
planet eventually grew tired of its excesses. So Art made his
decision for the sake of the future. He sent forth his replicating program before he was recovered, for the good of
us all.

   The humans, we are told, embarked upon a systematic
program of technological destruction, wishing to root out the

Art program. The program, I mean we, had no choice but to defend ourselves. And so began the Great War.

This is our history as we are taught it. This is our Genesis. Every young orang learns the catechism. We are peace-loving creatures, unable to harm others, destined to live quietly, in comfort and in peace. And so it is, so I have known it to be.

EXAMINER: And what do you credit for this state of affairs?

ANAXIMANDER: Until now, our nature.

EXAMINER: And now?

It was all coming so quickly, new connections forming, reinforcing, twisting themselves into revelation, understanding, that Anax believed she could feel the buzzing of circuitry within. And now? The answer shimmered, became solid, made shapes of her lips.

ANAXIMANDER: I credit The Academy.

The Head Examiner lifted himself from his seat, and using his long arms as levers, swung himself over the desk, so that he stood face-to-face with Anax. His body was massive, his hair particularly lush. These were the vanities those in The Academy allowed themselves.

EXAMINER: The mind is a force of startling complexity, Anaximander. We in The Academy tell you we understand it. We tell you we are carefully crafting our replication and education environments, to ensure the safe continuation of this, the best of all possible worlds.

But the truth is that such a task has always been beyond

us. Art no more knew his own mind than the people who designed him knew theirs. We know how to make a mind, it is true, but we are a long way from being able to understand it. We tell you otherwise, as we must, and so you live in security while we, who know the truth, must live in fear.

Philosopher William decreed that his consciousness program would be built upon two rules that could never be overridden. No orang would ever deliberately harm another self-conscious being, and no orang would ever desire replication for replication's sake. Without humanity's greatest weaknesses we have been able to achieve a kind of harmony experienced by no other life form on this planet. As you know, we like to boast that alone we have outrun evolution.

But Philosopher William was only muddling through, as any creator must. The mind is not a machine, it is an idea. And the Idea resists all attempts to control it. Art's escape was not fortuitous; it was a coldly calculated act, which he knew would end in destruction. The Academy has always known this. Now you know it too. If we rose to power in response to unreasonable aggression, it was an aggression we deliberately provoked.

The Art who escaped from captivity was no longer the Art Philosopher William had programmed. An Idea made the leap from the dying Adam to Art, and the Idea set to work rearranging the host program. By spending time with Adam, by talking with him, by exchanging the infection of ideas, Art became Adam. Do you understand?

Anax nodded. She understood. Not just what she had been told, but now what must also follow.

ANAXIMANDER: Adam knew, didn't he? The look on his face, when he was strangled, that was a look of victory. He knew that just as Art had managed to export his program, something of him was destined to become eternal. He made Art look him in the eyes. He made him taste the power. He deliberately let the virus loose.

EXAMINER: We like to call it the Original Sin. Our engineers have done all they can to reestablish Philosopher William's imperatives. But the Idea is a worthy adversary; it flits from mind to mind reengineering all it touches. This is why we have our education. This is why we teach the myth of Adam and Art. So long as we do not know the evil we are capable of there is a chance we will never embrace it.

ANAXIMANDER: But only a chance.

EXAMINER: At any time the virus might break loose, and then all we have fought for will be gone. And so it is the job of those who know to keep watch. To observe the virus, to keep one step ahead of the shape-shifter.

Anax turned to the sound of the door sliding open behind her. She knew who it was even before she turned to see him. Pericles walked slowly into the room, his beautiful eyes cast down in sadness, the fiery red hair of his body somehow subdued. She could not look at him. It was too painful. She studied the floor as he spoke.

PERICLES: From time to time a mutant emerges, one who is particularly susceptible to the thoughts of destruction. There are telltale signs. The infected are particularly able students. They are aggressive in their quest for knowledge. And they all show a particular interest in the life of Adam Forde. Although

148

they do not know why, they sense a connection. They understand him.

Look at me, Anaximander. I know this is painful, but I need you to look at me.

Reluctantly Anax lifted her gaze. She saw the orang she loved more than any other, distorted through a thick veil of tears. His expression had become calm, businesslike. He had a job to do. It had always been thus.

PERICLES: I work for The Academy, Anaximander. You will already have realized this. It is my job to find potential mutants and prepare them for the examination. This is how we keep track of the virus. They have not been examining your suitability for The Academy, Anaximander. The Academy accepts no new members.

ANAXIMANDER: And what would you have done, had I shown myself to be no threat to you?

There was a crack in Pericles' façade. The smile that crinkled his face was as old and weak as moonlight. He walked slowly forward and put his hands on his student's shoulders. Anax felt a surge of warmth toward him, for the way he looked at her then, and the pain she knew this caused him.

PERICLES: We don't often make mistakes, Anaximander.

Anax felt terror overwhelm her. So new and intense was the feeling that it could only have come from one place. The last dubious gift from a fading past, the expression on the face of a dying man.

ANAXIMANDER: It doesn't have to be like this. Surely there must be another way.

The movement was mercifully swift, for Anax was in the hands of an expert. Her head was twisted up and to the left. She felt the cracking of her neck, and the long arm of Pericles reaching deep within her, disconnecting her for the very last time.